Some Sort of Normal

Some Sort of Normal

Richard M. Grove

First Edition

Hidden Brook Press
www.HiddenBrookPress.com
writers@HiddenBrookPress.com

Copyright © 2019 Hidden Brook Press
Copyright © 2019 Richard Grove

All rights for story and characters revert to the author. All rights for book, layout and design remain with Hidden Brook Press. No part of this book may be reproduced except by a reviewer who may quote brief passages in a review. The use of any part of this publication reproduced, transmitted in any form or by any means, electronic, mechanical, photocopied, recorded or otherwise stored in a retrieval system without prior written consent of the publisher is an infringement of the copyright law.

This book is a work of fiction. Names, characters, places and events are either products of the author's imagination or are employed fictitiously. Any resemblance to actual events, locales or persons, living or dead, is entirely coincidental.

Some Sort of Normal
by Richard M. Grove

Cover Design – Richard M. Grove
Layout and Design – Richard M. Grove

Typeset in Garamond
Printed and bound in Canada
Distributed in USA by Ingram,
    in Canada by Hidden Brook Distribution

Library and Archives Canada Cataloguing in Publication

Grove, Richard M. (Richard Marvin), 1953-, author
    Some sort of normal / Richard M. Grove. -- First edition.

Issued in print and electronic formats.
ISBN 978-1-927725-63-4 (softcover).--ISBN 978-1-927725-64-1 (ebook)

    I. Title.

PS8563.R75S66 2018   C813'.54   C2018-906634-2
                          C2018-906635-0

for the harmed innocent

Contents

Chapters:

1 – You Had Better Start Praying – *p. 3*
2 – Therapy Excerpt – Stolen Innocence – *p. 10*
3 – Four Years Earlier, Conversation with Harrison – Some Sort of Normal – *p. 15*
4 – Therapy Excerpt – Beige – *p. 18*
5 – Mary and Her Girlfriend Co-Workers – *p. 24*
6 – Therapy Excerpt – Commitment – *p. 27*
7 – Therapy Excerpt – Wheelbarrows Full of Horseshit – *p. 30*
8 – Therapy Excerpt – The Other Skeleton in the Closet – *p. 34*
9 – Coffee with Frank – A Lecture from Frank – *p. 40*
10 – Therapy Excerpt – Prepubescent Sexualization – *p. 44*
11 – Bottle of Scotch Talking – *p. 47*
12 – Coffee with Frank – "Spotlight" – *p. 52*
13 – Therapy Excerpt – A Good Girl She Was – *p. 56*
14 – It's All Just a Bunch of Psychobabble – *p. 59*
15 – Coffee with Frank – Celebrate the Beauty of the Naked Child – *p. 63*
16 – Coffee with Frank – What's this Business about the Burkinis? – *p. 68*
17 – A Thread of Emails from Brother Harrison – *p. 72*
18 – Therapy Excerpt – Father was a bit of a Tough Cookie – *p. 76*
19 – Therapy Excerpt – The Fly Sucked Dry by the Spider – *p. 78*
20 – Therapy Excerpt – The Reluctant Pedophile – *p. 81*
21 – Letters to Brother Mark – *p. 83*
22 – 2 Emails to Michael from Harrison – *p. 89*
23 – Therapy Excerpt – 800 Years of Temptation – *p. 91*
24 – Therapy Excerpt – Mother – *p. 95*

25 – Coffee with Frank – Leonard Cohen and Donald
   Trump in the Same Sentence? – *p. 99*
26 – Therapy Excerpt – Thanksgiving – *p. 103*
27 – Therapy Excerpt – Peanut Butter and Banana Sandwich – *p. 109*
28 – Letter 4 from Brother Harrison – *p. 115*
29 – Coffee with Frank – Tick Tick Tick – *p. 117*
30 – Therapy Excerpt – The Top Drawer – *p. 120*
31 – Email to Family from Harrison – *p. 124*
32 – The Metamorphosis of Mark Beetleman – *p. 127*

Four scholarly analyses for book club analysis.
   – A Journey into the Dark – *p. 137*
   – From *Living in the Shadow* to *Some Sort of Normal* – *p. 141*
   – ungeheures ungeziefer – *p. 146*
   – More To Think About – *p. 146*

A Quick Bio Note – *p. 156*

*All crimes,
from stealing a dime, a tv, or a car,
all the way to sexual exploitation and rape
are all the result of feeble
justifications and rationalizations
by the offender.*

*Such reasoning
is deeply rooted in the notion
that the perpetrator
does not feel loved by God.*

Chapter 1

You Had Better Start Praying

A thin breeze filtered through yellowing October. Dry leaves chattered their way across the terrazzo floor into the corner. Mark Beetleman and his good friend Frank sat in the only sunny corner of the almost deserted patio bar.

"It's frickin' hot sitting here in the sun, even if it is late October," Mark complained. "Don't you feel hot man? You even have a sweater on."

"It's not all that hot." Frank replied.

Mark wiped beads of perspiration from his brow as he reeled nervously in the sweating tropics of his troubled mind. "Feels bloody hot to me."

Frank peered over his paper past his black-rimmed reading glasses at his friend. "You don't look so good. You sick or something?"

"No, not sick. Well, yeah, kind of sick I guess but not like what you're thinking. It's like I'm living a nightmare that I can't shake. I'm always on pins and needles these days." Mark scratched at his short, trimmed beard with both hands and whipped his sleeve across his brow.

"Let me guess. You're sick of your dead-end job that you hate but you're still worried that you might get canned? That dichotomy would make anyone sick, for Pete's sake."

Frank shook his head. "That tiny-minded boss of yours, those are your words buddy not mine, is finally getting to you? You keep saying that you have had enough of your job as copy editor and facts checker but you hang on to your job like a dog with a bone. I bet you're wishing you had stuck it out to become a lawyer after all this malarkey? It's never too late to go back to school buddy."

Mark wiped another eruption of perspiration from his brow. "Frank, don't you ever get depressed with life and wonder why you bother sticking around?"

"What the heck buddy." Frank looked startled. "What do you mean by that?"

Mark hesitated. Squirming in his seat he said, "Yah, I still hate my job and it used to be that all I had to worry about was feeling trapped in my six-by-six cubicle. I realized that even my stupid goldfish looked happier than me. Sometimes I feel like that thing is smarter than I am because he just swims around and stopped fighting the barriers of his glass walls. But now, well..."

Mark fell silent and took a long quaff of his drink.

"Now well what?" Frank sounded impatient.

Mark took a deep breath and said, in an almost whisper, "Listen. What if I told you I'd done something—something considered the fuckin' worst. Would you disown me?"

Frank put down his paper, took off his glasses and gave an incredulous laugh. "Don't tell me that you've gone and killed one of your ex-wives?" Frank laughed again, "And you buried her in your backyard."

"Fuck man, get serious." Mark looked away.

"For heaven sake Mark." The whirr of busy downtown

traffic forced Frank to raise his voice. "What in heck is going on with you?"

"Holy Shit man, keep it down." Mark's voice dropped to a whisper. He leaned forward just a bit closer to Frank. He felt nauseous, but he knew he had to let his old friend in on his deep secret. "Listen man, I could go to jail."

Frank was staring at him. "What the hell have you done? Is this some kind of joke?"

"No joke man." Mark hung his head. "I don't want to tell you right now, too many people around. But listen, I'll understand if you never want to speak to me again."

Mark couldn't bear to sit there any longer, not with Frank's eyes burning into him like that. A cold breeze whispered by. He suddenly felt chilled to the bones. He got up abruptly and trudged off to the bathroom.

* * *

Mark sat back hard in his chair. In a whisper Mark looked over his shoulder, rubbed his bristly face in his hands and spilled the beans to Frank. Silence fell heavy between the two of them. Mark sat pale-faced.

Frank leaned forward and stared him straight in the eye. Lowering his voice he said, "Holy... fricken... heck..., pardon my French but that is one heck of a bombshell to drop on me.

Frank ran his fingers through his short blond hair. "My head is spinning and I can't imagine what you have been going through let alone what the heck your daughters are going through. What the heck am I supposed to think let alone say? I hate to add fuel to your worry buddy but I have seen enough jailhouse movies to know that you wouldn't last for five minutes in jail. It's no wonder that you are sweating bullets man. Before you know it, you would be beaten to a pulp and you'd end up as someone's bitch."

The traffic quieted, Frank slumped back in his chair and lowered his voice. "There are no secrets in jail man. A friend of mine used to be a security guard in a State pen. He told me that the guards would for sure tell an inmate and the word would be out in a flash. Whether the system or the inmates like it or not, the guards control the flow of information and information is power. If a guard wants to see an inmate done in or just made to bend over, all they have to do is leak some information that will do him harm. I hate to say it quite like this but once they find out what you did, you would be as good as strung up."

A painful silence throbbed between them.

"You had better start praying buddy. You know that it's not just your daughter that could call the police. You had better hope that her mother or even her grandmother don't report you. Once a report has been made there is probably not much that could stop that locomotive from derailing, crashing and burning your entire life. I worry for you Mark."

Mark crossed his arms and huffed, "That's just what I need is you telling me that I have plenty to worry about. It is no wonder I am depressed. It used to be that all I was depressed about was you nattering at me like some old hen about how I've gotta change my life and that I think too much about women and sex and I need to find someone to love and settle down with."

Mark huffed again and continued with his diatribe as he squirmed in his padded armchair. "Don't bug me and tell me that I'm trapped in my little life of solitude and have to get out more and then give me your fuckin' comment that my life is a crashing train. It is no wonder that I'm depressed."

Mark squinted at Frank, "As far as sex goes, you are just jealous because I have more great sex in a weekend than you do in six months. Feeding me this jail and guard stuff is just your way of sidetracking the real issue that you are jealous."

Mark's face flushed as the traffic noise, once again, dropped off to silence. Embarrassed that everyone was now turned looking at him he wondered how much had they heard? Leaning forward he pushed his face closer to Frank. In an almost whisper Mark hissed, "I don't want to hear anything more about guards and jail and police. It used to be that all I had to worry about was feeling trapped by my dead-end job."

Frank feigned a laugh and interrupted, "Like you said even your stupid goldfish looks happier than you."

"Don't make fun of my shit life, man." Mark wiped another eruption of perspiration from his brow. "Frank, don't you ever get depressed with life and wonder why you bother sticking around? Sure, sure, I figure that as long as my inbox is cleared and my copy edits are done by the end of the day my tiny-minded boss is happy. If he is happy then I am happy."

Frank laughed out loud, "You know the saying, 'happy wife, happy life', well in your case it's 'happy boss, happy life.'"

Mark followed with a half-smile, "Empty inbox, happy life." His smile quickly faded. "Isn't that enough? It should be enough. You are right Frank about your worries that my life might crash and burn at any bloody moment."

Mark stared for a few seconds at his drink on the table, his fourth whisky on the rocks, as if still trying to fathom it all, "I know you have read 'Brave New World' by Huxley. Sometimes I wish I had a 'Soma' quota at the end of the workday to carry me until the morning alarm. Hell maybe another to get me through the day. Heck I've wondered what it would be like to go on a nice long soma holiday and just never wake up. You wouldn't even know that you were dead."

Mark tried to fake a smile, "First I would fuck my brains out with Ingrid. She was a good lay as long as we were nowhere that her husband would find us and we were both half cut. We would take our last soma tabs and just never wake up."

Frank interjected, "That sounds weird and too scary to me, 'and just never wake up' that sounds more like the title of Chandler's novel, 'The Big Sleep'. I couldn't imagine let alone contemplate it."

"It doesn't sound weird to me at all," Mark piped in, "The way I feel these days, the big sleep sounds just fine. I am tired of my life and I am so tired of living in fear that my daughter might someday report me to the police."

Mark's face went pale. Reaching for his drink, he swigged his glass empty and plunked it hard on the table. Mark shrugged and picked at a small hole in the tablecloth and continued. "I don't know, maybe you're right. Maybe, I should get out more and get out of my head. I don't know what happened. Lately I've been peering out of my little aquarium wondering what I'm missing. Jim and Mary are heading to Jamaica for a holiday in February. You and Dorothy just got back from England and here I am, year after year, just making sure my in-box is clear by the end of the day."

Frank laughed, "Empty in-box, happy life."

"It's been going on like this for too long and you wonder why I am addicted to old episodes of 'Friends'. I don't know. I'm too depressed to even think about it most of the time, let alone to do anything about it."

Mark shifted his chair even further to the left and rambled on; Frank sipped his drink in silence, his head still spinning. More traffic rumbled by. Instead of raising his voice to compete, he just shut up and settled back into his seat. The shadows of the afternoon slowly, inevitably, crawled up the side of the checkered tablecloth and across the table. Neither Mark, nor Frank, spoke for the longest time. A cold breeze shivered them to pay their tab and move on.

Chapter 2

Therapy Excerpt – Stolen Innocence

Mark nodded and mumbled a bashful hello to his therapist, Dr. Waleed. As he settled into his chair he pulled a piece of paper from his pocket and unfolded it. "You keep suggesting that I write a journal of my thoughts and bring them once a week but just because I'm a copy editor and fact checker for a publishing company doesn't mean I'm a writer but here is a poem that I wrote just to bring in and share with you. It's not very good but at least I tried. Maybe I will write more, one day. Sorry I don't have a title yet."

> I wasn't always who I am today,
> despised by many, loved by none.
> I don't know how it is
> I got to be this person.
> Other than inch by inch
> I slipped down a slippery slope,
> or was I pushed
> or maybe dragged unwillingly.

One thing that I did
was that I willingly put on my blinders
and only thought of myself.
When I started to do that
I don't remember?

God give me the strength
to carry the claw-hooked dragon
that attached itself to my back.
Give me the knowledge
of how to pull it off
and suffer the scars.

It's not much but I tried. My brother Harrison is the writer in the family. He has written tons of poems and stories and even books and even had them published so I thought I would bring this other poem that he wrote about me. It is way better than mine that I just read. He wrote it about ten years ago about me when I was about seven."

Before Mark started to read, Dr. Waleed commented. "Thanks very much for sharing your poem Mark. It is a brave start for you. There is a lot in that poem for us to talk about. That is exactly why I wanted you to write and bring it in. Do you have a copy of it that I can have for my file? I would like to read it later and we can talk about it next week.

"It sounds like you are kind of proud of your brother Harrison and his accomplishments as a writer. Do you ever tell him that you are proud? Is that why you don't think of yourself as a writer because you feel you could never live up to what you think of him?"

Mark folded his paper back onto his lap. "He's a good writer and I am a bad writer and that's all there is to it. He is a pretty good guy all-round and I am not such a good guy but the reason that I wanted to read you his poem is because he saw that I was once a tender innocent little boy. I was even loved. I can't say that about me now but anyway here is his poem."

A Journey into the Dark

My little brother Mark
held my hand firm
in the now cool evening
of September.
"Don't be a sissy boy." I said.
"Mark, come with me.
Let me show you the stars."

We walked away
from the bright lights
of the front porch
into the dark
toward the open sky.
Silver stripes of dew painted
our naked legs as we walked
through the uncut grass
at the edge of the lawn
down into the distant hay-field
north past the lane.

This was territory little Mark
had not yet ventured into
during the day
let alone at night.
I was the brave 13-year-old big brother,
Mark was 6 years younger
clinging close to my side
into the dark to see the brilliant sky
in a way that his tender innocence
had not yet been revealed to him.

Mark shuffled in his chair and sat on his hands, "It's funny. Mostly I don't remember even living on the farm but I do remember being afraid of walking away from the house into the dark. I was about seven at the time and Jimmy was about four or maybe five. It was kind of nice that Harrison held my hand and took me to the fence to show me the other side of the universe. He knew I was just an innocent little kid and kind of afraid of the dark and afraid of being eaten by a bear or wolf or something."

Dr. Waleed spoke up. "One might have to argue the point that you stole that same innocence from your daughter. That same innocence that you once had but from what I am understanding is that you are not 100% convinced of that."

Dr. Waleed paused. "Am I right?"

Another pause. "Mark, it is not a rhetorical question. Am I right to think that it is no big deal that you stole your daughter's innocence and that you would say that her innocence and gaining it back is up to her not you or anyone."

Another pause. "Correct me if I am wrong but I think you

said something last week that innocence is in the eye of the beholder and you wonder if it is an actual quality that can be lost or lost forever."

"Yes I said something like that. I think that I was saying was that I had heard the term, 'born again virgin' and it made me think that if a virgin can be born again then I guess their virginity has not been totally lost like my innocence or my daughter's innocence and it can be born again. How did I lose my innocence? If I am to blame for the loss of my daughter's innocence then can it be born again? If so then I would think that it would be her responsibility to gain it back again."

Chapter 3

Four Years Earlier, Conversation with Harrison – Some Sort of Normal

Mark and Harrison lay in the shade at the edge of the small cliff looking over the vastness of the lake. The family hubbub of a squirt gun fight raged behind them. The breeze was delightfully cool. Mark sat up from looking at the drifting clouds and broke the silence that settled like warm sun between them. "Harrison, are you awake?"

"Of course I'm awake"

Mark rolled to his side, "We were just normal kids weren't we? Weird family but some sort of normal kids. I think we all grew up kind of normal but who really knows what lurks below the surface? We even fought like normal kids."

Harrison laughed and threw a fist full of grass at Mark. "I know I was kind of normal but I'm not so sure about you." Harrison flinched as one of the kids leaped over him with squirt guns blazing. "Mark, I don't know how normal we were but I remember one time when I threw a small piece of wood at you, who knows why? I was just being weird or something. It was kind of like throwing a stone at a bird but not really expecting to hit it and you never do but it hit you right between the eyes and it cut open your forehead and you bled like a stuck pig. You squealed like one too you sissy."

Mark sat up and interjected, "yah I remember. Mother sent Jimmy out to see what the ruckus was all about. He came running from the house thinking that you must have tried to kill me with an axe or something."

"Yah and you were crying and there was so much blood. You got blood all over your hands and all over your shirt and up the wall on the way in the house. Dripping spots led a path all the way to the bathroom."

"I can hardly remember all of that." Mark said as he sat up. "I only remember because you, or someone, had told the story so many times. It's weird what we remember and what we don't."

Harrison said, "Oh man I remember only too well, you howled like a wounded dog. All I wished was that you would just shut up and stop your screaming. Later on our neighbor, Miss Milly, said that she almost called for an ambulance you were screaming so loud. You wouldn't have known it was just a little scratch and didn't even need stitches."

"I remember everyone was pissed off at you for days. Ma kept sayin', 'Harrison, it could have been so much worse. Harrison, you could have put an eye out. Harrison, don't you think before you act?' Brother, you paid for that big time."

Harrison replied "Yah I guess we were pretty normal kids. We used to bike all over the place. The three of us. Jim was the youngest so I tied a rope from my bike to his and I towed him around where ever we went. Sometimes we would take a pack of wieners with us and make a fire down at the creek and stay all afternoon swimming and lying in the sun."

"Yah I remember those days." Mark said with a slight smile. "Yah, I guess we were some sort of normal."

"Do you remember the time when we biked all the way up to cousin Bobby's house and I towed Jimmy up the hill at the water reservoir? We all bulleted down the other side like mad demons and I didn't think to disconnect Jimmy before heading down. I whipped out at the bottom and poor Jimmy came flyin' like a bat out of hell and landed right on top of me and my bike. His bike landed right on my nuts; I thought that I was going to die. I was so bruised and hurtin' I decided to call dad to come and get us but he was too drunk to drive. He told me to 'F' off and told me that if I could get us there then I could get us back. We walked all the way home. Man was I sorry I ever pulled that stunt."

Mark slapped his hands on his legs and laughed out loud. "I always wondered why we were walking our bikes home. I remember now, you just kept telling me to shut up and keep walkin'. By the time we got home it was dark and we all just went to bed."

Harrison fell back onto the grass. "Those were the days of innocence man. Those were the days of some sort of normal alright. We were just normal kids doing normal things. Now that we are adults we have so much to worry about and how we can give our kids that same life of blameless innocence. Those were the good old days."

Harrison and Mark lay in silence in the long shadows of the late afternoon for the longest time.

Chapter 4

Therapy Excerpt – Beige

Mark Beetleman sat in his therapist's office with is hands on his lap waiting for Dr. Waleed to look up from shuffling papers. Dr. Waleed slapped his folder closed and spryly said. "So Mark. How was your week?"

It was obviously a rhetorical question. The doctor, without even a half a second pause, said, "You have been coming to see me for almost two years now. I was just looking at my notes," He patted the folder on his lap, "and I realized that I had never asked you who you think you are. If you were going to write a letter to describe yourself to some respected moral leader, someone like Martin Luther King, or Gandhi, or even Jesus if you like, how would you describe yourself to them?

Mark was taken aback. He fumbled with a folded paper that he had brought with him to read. With a stammer he lurched into an unenthusiastic reply. "Well… Well, I don't know… I guess I would say that I have a short, trimmed beard," He scratched at his chin, "and thinning brown hair and I'm kind of good-looking but not very muscular like some buff guys are."

Dr. Waleed scratched at his own chin and said, "Let's forget the physical description stuff and describe who you really are. Tell me something essential about yourself."

Mark squirmed and put the folded paper into his shirt pocket, "Well... I guess I would say that I was just a normal guy with normal interests, from a normal family with normal hang-ups. Well I guess I am kind of normal but I guess that's for you to say, not me. Some probably wouldn't even describe me with brown hair with a beard. They would describe me as being beige", Mark put his hands over his head and made air quotes around the word 'beige'. "I guess I would have to say that I am a self-confessed, paranoid, germophobe, and Frank thinks that I have a dry, colorless imagination. This pretty much sums me up, beige and colorless. How normal is all of this? I've no idea."

Mark looks up at Dr. Waleed half expecting an answer but continues while he fumbled for the paper that he had just put back in his pocket. "I brought in something that I printed out after I sent it to Frank if you want me to read it. I brought it because I think it says a lot of who I am. I was going to read it to you." Mark laughed, "Jesus or Gandhi can probably figure out how I am if they want to listen in.

Mark paused and fumbled with his paper. "I guess my mother and three ex-wives would for sure describe me as beige. My mother constantly complained about the clothes I wore even as far back as when I was a young boy. No matter how she tried to jazz up my color choices I still gravitated to the same beige and gray choices that weaseled their way into my closet. My mother always tried her best to work me out of my drab persona by presenting a colorful cardigan for Christmas, a red shirt for my birthday but nothing seemed to make an impact. 'Different shades of gray and beige don't count as color choices,' she said time and time again.

"Many years later, after my mom died, my ex-wife, Mary, a flamboyant redhead that loved color, berated me with a daily mantra reminding me that beige was not only the color of my wardrobe, and apartment, but even more, my entire personality. Needless to say, that marriage lasted all of five minutes. Despite the hurtful rejection, I longed for her and offered to change. I was a sorry mess when she left me. I pleaded with her and showed up at her door wearing gray flannel pants and a beige shirt with a darker beige stripe incorporated into what I thought was a risqué loud pattern of disturbance. I loved her, I was committed and I wanted to show her I was willing to change for her; for the sake of our marriage, for our future children I was willing to wear any colors she wanted me to wear.

"It was at that time that I discovered the utter futility of trying to change my personality. You can change a leopard's spots but it is still a leopard. It is the deep-down core of a person that makes them this way or that and I was, whether I liked it or not, Beige.

"I read something one time that said, 'Analyze your dreams and you will see the true color of your soul.' I discovered that I also dreamt in beige rather than in black and white like most so-called, normal people. It was my delight when I stepped out of the beige persona, even if only, subconsciously in a dream.

"Let me read you an email that I sent to Frank after a dream I had the other night."

Email Subject Heading: i dreamt in color last night

frank, u'll never guess what but i hd a dream in color last night. i can't remember when, if ever, i dreamed in color maybe never. everything is always in beige; sky, trees, grass, me and my clothes all in beige but this dream was in color, everything was in color. it was amazing. the trees were bright green ad the sky was a color of blue that i had never seen before but the funny thing is that it was night and all of the buildings were gray and the streets were gray but i was walking down the street, down the middle, there were no cars or anything anywhere but then when i got to the intersection i was standing waiting and waiting for the light to turn green. It stayed this brilliant red for the longest time and finally when i decided to cross the street against the red light there were four girls, maybe half of my age, pretty and they all had long beige hair, kind of like you see in movies but not as golden more beige than blond and as i was about to cross the street, even though the light was still red, one of the girls yells out, 'there is one don't let him get away' and they started to run towards me so i started to run away and eventually they caught up to me even though i was running as fast as i could they threw me down in the middle of the street and started to make love to me in a vicious kind of way and not one at a time man but all at the same time. i was naked and they were naked and their breasts rubbed all over me and their beige hair was dangling in my face as we made love. we were just one big ball of intertwined beige bodies embroiled in a steamy ultimate release and then eventually i lay there exhausted and the girls were gone and everything turned back to black and white. AND THEN I WOKE UP!!!!!!!!!!!!!!! and i had to pee real bad but i couldn't until the swelling went down and then I just sat on the side of my bed and laughed and laughed. i don't know if my neighbors could hear me laughing at three in the morning or not but i just laughed and laughed. Man i needed that laugh.

btw give me a call and let me know how your trip went.

ttys mark

"After I clicked send I wondered what Sigmund Freud would say about that dream". Mark gave a half laugh again. "Let alone what Gandhi and Jesus would say. I don't know if I ever told you but I took a psych 101 class back in my university days. I started wondering what it all meant. What on earth does beige hair mean? Was I aroused by the beige banality of my own sexuality? The abandoned intersection, traveling from nowhere, to nowhere, arriving nowhere, ravaged by the unattainable yet ultimately abandoned, waking to the reality of disappointment, waking to aloneness, raped, used – even if momentarily willing, even if encouraging. Why were the girls only half my age? That made them pretty young teenagers? If Freud was right then I was not just the ravaged but the ravager. I was not just myself or even just the girls but it was also the streets, empty. I was the long stoplight that never turned green, I was the lost, desolate city, gray and then as I pondered the hidden psychological meanings my chuckles of delight turned to despair.

"Well, by then I was wide awake and in no mood to go back to sleep so I slipped on a pair of my old tattered moccasin slippers that I had mended with silver duct tape. It was a nice night but I was hit by the chilly air as I stepped off the back deck into the dark night. Dew covered everything. Stars filled the sky like I had never seen before. I walked out to the quiet streets of Gary, Indiana and meandered aimlessly in the direction of flashing neon. It was really quiet, almost dead. I nodded to Mario flipping some pizza dough in the window of 'Mama Gino's'. I wandered past the wine store, past the Goodwill secondhand store where most of my drab wardrobe was carefully selected.

"I stopped in front of 'Nicky's Second-Hand Wonders' and wondered if they had ever sold an LP from their twenty-five cent sale bin. It is funny but I stared at myself in the window. All of a sudden there were no cars, no bikes, no traffic noise of any kind. I smirked; I was in the abandoned city of my nightmare looking past my beige shirt to the dull gray of privation. I flinched back into reality as the traffic light turned green bringing the sounds of the city gently back to life; traffic droned, silencing the clinking of my generosity, coins tossed into the hat of a street person, slumped; snoring echoed in the hollow door well. Without stopping, I ambled home exhausted, hoping I could return to sleep.

Mark slumped back in his chair. "Sorry I rambled on so much and I know we are just about out of time but what do you think of my dream? And don't you dare just turn it back on me and ask what I think. I already told you what I think. I want to know what you think. I just want to know how normal I am, that's all. And I just want to know how messed up I am."

Chapter 5

Mary and Her Girlfriend Co-Workers

Mark's ex-wife Mary sat at the lunch table with her girlfriend co-workers. "You think that your husband is bad just because he says to his buddies that he had to 'baby sit' his own kids as if they weren't his own and he was doing you a big favor. My first husband Mark didn't even want kids when he was with me let alone baby sit them."

They ignored the clatter of the cafeteria as they leaned into the plate of French fries they were sharing.

"You think your husband is a bore just because he likes to talk about cars and work. Mark was more than boring. His mother, God rest her soul, and I used to tease him by calling him Mr. Beige. Believe me, Mark was Mr. Boring. You have nothing to complain about girl."

Mary forked a French fry and dipped it into the catsup. "You should have seen him. Every morning was the same old thing. The same gray pants, polish his shoes and then he'd start complaining about "the damn Gary Indiana Transit System". Every morning he would say the same thing, "I hate the GIT. It is one of my least favorite places to spend time," he would say.

Then he would whine, "Not only don't I like where it is taking me every morning but I frickin' disliked the jammed proximity of sharing space and air with anyone, let alone total strangers." Every morning he would grumble about the same thing. "People, they take up too much space and use up all the air in the bus."

Between breaths Mary stuffed another French fry into her mouth and continued, not giving anyone any opportunity to jump in with their own complaints.

"It's crazy to say but he was the same with both of his other ex-wives as he was with me. We all eventually took up too much of what he called 'his' private space. I don't know why but he never learned how to comfortably share a bed or even a sofa, let alone air space with any of us. I am amazed he ever had kids. I got to know his other ex-wives and we compared notes." Mary waved a skewered French fry at her girlfriends. "They both said that soon after they got married he grew less and less tolerant of what he called 'obligatory snuggle time' even while watching TV."

Mary's girlfriend Sue brushed aside her long blond hair and jumped in, "You are lucky now though. You said that your husband Donnie even likes to snuggle." Sue started to laugh, "And you said that he doesn't snuggle just because it is a prelude to sex. You lucky bitch. You are going to make us all sick with envy."

Mary laughed while she gritted her teeth. "Yah, I'm lucky to be with Donnie now. It used to be that every cocktail party we ever went to Mark would hang out with a couple of guys in a far corner and say that there was an axiom of life that he always advocated and that is that women liked to snuggle and men liked to have sex.

Mary puffed out her chest and said in a manly voice. 'Men tolerate snuggle time only for the reward of sex and women tolerate sex for the reward of snuggle time.' It was like he had this shtick that he always turned to with a bunch of guys." Mary laughed out loud. Thank God I dumped him.

"I know I badmouth Mark but he's not all bad and at least he is not afraid of commitment so much that he can't take care of his own daughters. They are lucky to have him. From what I understand their mother is downright nuts. She is lucky that she didn't wake up dead one morning buried in a deep hole in the backyard."

The girlfriends all laughed about waking up dead. They sat poking at their plate of fries. Each of them taking turns at shredding their husbands or boyfriends. Each of their diatribes sounded much the same as each other's. Lunch just wouldn't be the same without complaining about the men in their lives.

Chapter 6

Therapy Excerpt – Commitment

Mark was riled up. He looked straight at Dr. Waleed. "If I was so afraid of commitment and such an unloving person you might wonder how it is that I ended up living with and taking care of my two daughters as a single father but you never asked me anything about that. Nobody does. What is it you want to talk about today? Forget about it. Let me tell you about my crazy wives. They weren't any sort of normal. One was a schizophrenic, manic-depressive; and one was an alcoholic, a total lush and had a secret past life as a stripper and hooker that she kept from me even when we were married; and one was just downright a crazy and controlling bitch that didn't give me a moment's peace of mind just to relax."

Mark rolled his eyes and shrugged his shoulders, "She browbeat me about leaving the toilet seat up or how I squeezed the toothpaste in the middle or if I left a bit of toothpaste in the sink that was f'in' hell warmed over. She bitched about me leaving my dirty socks at the end of the bed even if I picked them up in the morning. One time she flipped out, yelling at me because I put her toothbrush on the back of the toilet because that is not where you put a toothbrush that has to go in your mouth. She didn't want to know that I had picked it up off of the floor for her, from behind the toilet for F sake, she just threw it in the garbage. I would have loved to see her stick it in her mouth. I would have choked on my laugh if she had done that. Instead of letting her nag me to death I put a few of my things in a bag and just walked out one evening, right in the middle of a movie. I even remember the movie – When Harry Met Sally. She was nagging at me about something and I just walked out without saying a word."

Mark laughed. "I didn't even get to see Meg Ryan do her orgasm in the restaurant and the lady say. 'I'll have what she's having'. I never even went back. I never went back for any of my stuff. I felt like I was liberated or something." Mark's laugh quickly turned into a scowl followed by an audible huff.

"Yah – both of my daughters came from Rose. One week she was up and cheerful and loved cooking and cleaning and even loved sex but then the next week she was a slovenly bitch and accused me of raping her and called the police. She was just nuts. One week she would get a great job and a month or two later she would lose it because she couldn't get out of bed to go to work."

Mark dropped his eyes from Dr. Waleed and shook his head. "I tried to live with it for years but eventually she scared the girls one too many times. Up, down, up, down, up, down. It finally drove me and my daughters nuts so when I finally left her I took the girls and moved into a little one-bedroom apartment. When a judge finally gave me custody of the girls I got a bigger place and took care of them as a single dad. They were about four and six at the time and moved out only when they went off to college. It was an ok life at the time. I was on welfare and did just about everything for my girls. Rose got to see the girls every other weekend. Sometimes the girls and I would go to visit their grandmother - Nanna Dorie – is what they called her. She was an ok grandmother. She even helped me get custody of the girls because she knew how wacko Rose was. Now, of course, she hates my guts for what I did. She said she would cut off my nuts off if she ever saw me again. Never mind what a good father I was for all of those years."

Chapter 7

Therapy Excerpt – Wheelbarrows Full of Horseshit

"Hi Doc, sorry I mean Dr. Waleed. I don't know what you wanted to talk about this week but it seems every time I turn around I have another nightmare to tell you about. I didn't used to have nightmares, I wish they would stop. It was such an awful night. It was the middle of the night and I sat up stone cold in a sweat and swung my legs to the side of the bed and felt disoriented for the longest time. My shoulders were heavy and aching as I slumped my elbows to my knees and rubbed my eyes over and over again. It was really dark, usually there is at least a bit of light from the moon or street light or something but all I could see was the red haze that radiated from the bedside clock beaming 3:53 am and then it blinked 3:54. The last few minutes, or had it been hours, seemed so much like real life that I was disoriented. The confusion of this being a nightmare or memory fumbled in my brain as I struggled to consciousness. It was so weird."

"It was so weird that Harrison was in my nightmare." Mark

rubbed his eyes as if reliving the experience, "Why had Harrison been on the road with me? But there he was, clear as day, walking two paces in front of me. How on earth did I get stuck walking home behind him, my brother, who refuses to speak to me. I haven't even seen him in who knows how long. I haven't even spoken to him for a long time, I guess ever since he and the family found out about what I did with Rachel."

Mark involuntarily rubbed his eyes and the top of his head. He pulled a piece of paper out of his pocket. "I emailed it to Frank 'cause', I kind of, send him everything that is going on in my head." Mark started to read as if it were a story he found in a magazine.

Without turning to Mark, my brother pivoted in his tracks, slipped on a pair of pristine, white deerskin gloves, picked up the handles of his wheelbarrow and started, at a quick pace, to walk towards home. After a moment of hesitation I grabbed my white gloves, grasped the handles of my wheelbarrow and hurried to catch up.

Despite the fact that my brother had disowned me years ago, here I was trotting down the gravel road trying to catch up to him, both of us pushing wheelbarrows full of fresh, stinking horseshit. Still a few paces behind my brother, I wondered what the hell I was supposed to do? Break out into song, give my brother a cheery back smacking –"So how you doing bro?" I felt like saying "Hey you bastard, if I have to push this load of horseshit with you, you ARE going to tell me how you got in my dream and how you got to be such a sullen son-of-a-bitch with me. What the hell did I ever do to you to warrant pushing a wheelbarrow full of horse crap downwind from you?"

Mark shuffled his printout looking for the next page.

"A smirk came over my face with a subtle strategy. I would

let my pace slow, bit by bit. I would pull back and let more and more distance fall between me and my brother. I would play a game to see if my brother would even notice. The palpable quiet was interrupted only by the rhythmical squeaking of our wheelbarrows timed with the drumming of our footfalls."

Mark shuffled and crumpled his papers as if trying to stall. After a supportive nod from Dr. Waleed he continued. "The greater the distance that fell between me and my brother, the greater the relief of not having to share space with him, but still the stink of my own horseshit filled the path. In my dream I remember saying to myself, 'I have, for too many years, shared my life with him; I don't need to share another, single breath and smell the horseshit he is pushing around'.

"With every step, I wondered what was going through my brother's mind. My brother's normal aloof demeanor, his speechlessness is well rehearsed with years of silence under his belt. Whatever was going through his mind I have no idea but he walked in stoic silence, in an unvaried quick pace. I even remember, in my dream, saying out loud to myself, 'Thank God, I am finally alone.' my pace went slower and slower until I could finally slip, out of sight, behind a tree. If my brother were to turn around and look for me now I would have vanished, there would not even be a footprint in the dust behind him. There would not be the squeak of a wheel or even the shuffle of shoes on gravel. I simply would not be there".

From Mark's vantage point his brother does not turn to look where he is. His pace does not deviate. Mark mumbles out loud to himself. "Is he deaf? Did he forget that I was there? Does he have no imagination whatsoever? Maybe I fell behind him and was dying in the dust." Maybe that would not matter to his brother. Never did he turn, not even once to see or say anything. His steady pace was unwavering, unyielding.

Mark sat in the shade on the rim of his stinking wheelbarrow behind the tree. No brother in sight, sheltered from the penetrating sun he felt a sad, dry breeze blow the aroma of manure across the empty field. The stench of his own wheelbarrow was all-pervasive. Mark reached over and flicked off the night light. Rubbed his eyes and slumped back into bed. He pressed his head into his still hot pillow. There would be little sleep for him that night.

Mark slumped in the big wing-back chair and crossed his arms. "So there you go. That is my, pushing a wheelbarrow full of horseshit, story. I don't even want to know what you think of it. It is pretty obvious that I've been pushing my own stinkin' load of shit around while I try to make it back home and I think my brother has his own load of shit to deal with but he doesn't want to talk to me about it. All it makes me is tired."

Chapter 8

Therapy Excerpt – The Other Skeleton In the Closet

"Good afternoon Doc." With something of a vacuous smile Mark nodded his head at Dr. Waleed. With a bit of a chin pointed grumble he protested, "Why do we always have to get back to Rachel and Selene? What is so important about my relationship with my daughters that we have to hash things over and over again? Why is my relationship with them more important than my relationship with my brother, Harrison, who won't even talk to me and I figure hates me? Last week I told you about him and my dream about pushing a load of horseshit around in a wheelbarrow and now you just want to swing straight into talking about my daughters again. I don't feel like we've even finished talking about my brother and my horseshit dream. Don't you know enough about them yet?

"Before I tell you more about Rachel and Selene I want to tell you something more about Harrison that I didn't tell you last week because we ran out of time. It is more about the dream and him and me pushing the wheelbarrows full of horseshit. Well what I didn't tell you is that Harrison molested his daughter and went to jail. Yah that's real life shit, not part of the dream. That is the shit that he has been carrying around with him. That is why he doesn't want to talk to me now in real life and why he didn't want to talk to me in the dream while he was pushing his wheelbarrow full of horseshit, both of us with our lily white gloves on, noses in the air. There we were walking into the aroma of our own horseshit. Every step we took it was inevitable that we would be walking in the smell of our own shit and I was trying to keep up with him and he was ignoring me when I finally just let him go on without me.

"He doesn't want to talk with me in real life because he knows that he and I are too much alike. The fact is that he just got off of the slippery slope and didn't have sex with his daughter. Basically what he did was touch his daughter's nipples. Society says he molested her. I think he said twice, while he thought that she was asleep and then right after each time he put her limp sleeping hand on his penis. Both times while he thought that she was asleep. At least that is what he told me and I guess I believe him. He said he was so freaked out at what he did he never did it again and signed up to see a shrink. Then he went to jail for three weeks because it turns out she wasn't asleep and his daughter told her mom, his ex-wife, and she told a teacher and the teacher told the police. I think that the conviction was for 'sexual exploitation' or something like that. He swore it never happened again and I believe him about that too but now he is all high and mighty with me and he thinks that he is better than me because he didn't rape his daughter. He so called, 'just' touched her while he thought she was asleep. The fucker calls me a pedophile and he was just the same as me and now he is pushing the same wheelbarrow of horseshit as me. What I think is that the law said he molested his daughter and that is different than what happened between me and my daughter. We made love for years and it wasn't rape. Him, he's a bastard hypocrite because he actually took advantage of her while she was asleep.

"Yah I know you want me to get back to Rachel but I just had to tell you what really happened and what my dream was all about. With Rachel I don't remember how it started. Rachel wanted it and I wanted it and it just happened. She was horny and I was horny. What more does it take? It wasn't rape, we made love every time. It's not like I tied her up, beat her, threw her on the floor and fucked her up the ass like some moron hillbilly. I didn't rape her if that is what you're trying to get me to say. It was actually kind of tender and nice. I know society thinks that I raped her but actually I think that it is our limiting, constricted, anxiety-driven society that is fucked-up, not me.

"The first time we actually made love wasn't for quite a while after we both wanted it. It all happened because of the shower. Yah, the shower. One time I was in the shower with her washing her hair like we always did and she slipped or something and grabbed on to me around my waist so she wouldn't fall. Hot water was streaming over both of us, steam filled the room and I was suddenly overcome by how soft and sexy she was. I had never thought of her that way before. I really mean it. I never did. I started to wash her back while she was pressed up against me and I rubbed soap over her and up over her shoulders and she just stood there and let me wash her and I washed up her legs and between her legs and I washed her vagina and I put my finger partly inside her but she winced slightly with pain so I stopped. That was the first time that anything sex-like happened and that is all that happened. I got a hard-on but I tried to hide it from her. We got out of the shower and I wrapped her in a big towel, dried her hair and sent her off to get her and her sister dressed so we could all leave. That was when she was about twelve or so. I don't remember exactly.

"What do you mean what happened then? I just told you. Nothing. No, I didn't just leave then. Well yah. After she left and I locked the bathroom door I jerked off. I had a hard on. What of it. I jerked off, I shaved, I got dressed and we went out to meet their mother and grandma for dinner like we always did on a Sunday afternoon. The girls want to see their mom so I take them. I can't stand my fuckin' ex but I gotta take them and be as nice as pie to her. Delores is the girls' grandmother, they call her Nanna Dorie. She keeps saying to just be nice, be nice for the sake of the girls. It's all one big f-in' lie but I do it anyway. I lie so much about my f-in' ex-wife that I start thinking that I might actually like her and we should get back together again and then she opens her mouth and says some bone-head thing and calls me lazy in front of my girls and all I want to do is smack her but I never do. I was taught never to be violent to a girl. Everyone thinks that I am the lazy, stay-at-home dad sucking money from her wallet but nobody has any idea what I gotta put up with.

"Yah, ok back to Rachel. People think that I must have been raping her and just fuckin' her like you see on some violent TV cop show but that isn't what happened at all. I love Rachel, I love both my daughters. A few days later I gave both girls a shower again but I got out first because it was too crowded in there for three people. The girls like having a shower together so I just left them to play and get washed and yah before you ask, I jerked off in the bedroom while they were in the shower so they wouldn't catch me. I don't know why I had a hard-on but I just did and I jerked off.

"I don't know how many times I showered with them after that time but every time I had a shower just with Rachel I washed her hair and she put her arms around like she did the first time when she slipped. From then on I washed her hair and then her back and then I never stopped and she always liked it. She always let me wash her vagina. It used to turn her on. Yah, I put my finger in her all the way after a few times. She winced in the beginning but I knew she liked it because she never stopped me. She never even tried to stop me. She just opened her legs. It was like an invitation. I don't know how many times we had sex. It was maybe once a week for about six years. Sometimes twice a week. Sometimes once a month but it was never just sex, it was making love every time."

Dr. Waleed wrote a quick note before speaking. The moment of silence made Mark squirm. "Before we finish today's session I want you to write down a couple of words and take them home and think about them. Those two words are 'prepubescent sexualization'. They are quite a mouthful but I think that you are ready to start looking at that concept. Start by looking up those words and maybe google them and see what you come across. Make some notes and bring them with you. Those words will be a good place for us to start next week.

Let me finish with saying something about 'prepubescent sexualization' for you to think about. What do I mean by the sexualization of prepubescent girls? I simply mean that sexualization occurs when individuals are regarded as sex objects rather than as people. This happens when the person, and I am talking specifically about young girls here, when they are evaluated in terms of their physical characteristics and sexiness by adult men. Prepubescent sexualization takes place when a young girl is appraised or valued, as a sex object, by an individual, almost always an adult male. They see them as conquerable sex objects, a sex object to have whenever they want. I would like you to think about this in relation to how you must have been viewing your daughter or even both daughters even though you had sex with only your oldest daughter. How and why is it that you looked at your daughter as a sex object?

Chapter 9

Coffee with Frank – A Lecture from Frank

Mark and Frank sat in their favorite coffee shop, each leaning over a low-fat double cappuccino. Mark was boasting about his latest sexual conquest and how young and pretty she was.

Frank piped in, "I can't keep track of all of your exploits. Is this a new one since I saw you last week? June was her name or was it May. I can't remember. Her name might have been January, February or March for all I know. Just name them by the month that you slept with them and make my life easy. When the heck are you going to settle down with just one woman."

Mark put down his New Yorker and leaned towards Frank. "No this is a new chick, Mary or Betty or something like that. I can't remember the names of the ones that aren't keepers. You're thinking of Ingrid. I told you about Ingrid, the sexy motorcycle chick. She was a keeper but she and I split up a couple of weeks ago. Man, she was so hot. I must have told you that we split up."

"I remember now. Isn't she the one that dumped you for her husband? I can't believe it. I thought she had been talking about leaving him, getting a divorce and marrying you. That was two weeks ago and I thought that you were crushed."

"Yah I was crushed. I was crushed for days." Mark waved both hands over his head and smacked them down on the table. "I can't believe it. She can't tell me that sex was better with him than with me. She was awesome in the sack. Do you know how many of her footprints are on the ceiling of my van? Heck, I'm still crushed."

Frank groaned, "Didn't you say the husband was some sort of a dweeb and you couldn't stand him?"

With a half grin on his face Mark gloated, "I met him a few times at parties and BBQs. She could have been fucking me right under his nose and I swear he wouldn't notice. He had his nose buried too deep in his guns. He was a gunsmith and collector or something like that. He even showed me his workshop one time and his locked cabinet full of pistols and rifles and shotguns. All of those guns kind of made me nervous so maybe it is just as well that she went back to him."

"Weren't you going to buy his Harley from him? What happened to that?"

"Yah it was a nice bike and everything but basically I couldn't come up with the bread. Ingrid and I were going to ride together. She had a bright red Harley, a bit smaller than his. She looked so sexy in her black leathers.

"My girls even liked her. She treated them real well but I don't see my girls much these days since Rachel moved south to Indianapolis. From Gary to the Nap is just too far to go. I can hardly keep up the payments on the van let alone the extra gas."

Frank cautiously interrupted, "If you wanted to see your daughters you would see your daughters. The amount you spend on women would easily cover the cost of gas to see your daughters but let's face it Mark you are more interested in yourself than keeping things together with your daughters. Even your van, sex mobile, that it is, you should get rid of it. Your mom and dad are both gone and all you have is your daughters. The only reason you bought it is to have sex at the drop of a hat. Wise up man.

Frank put his hand up at Mark, "Don't interrupt me while I'm on a roll. You remember a couple of years ago I had a hankering to have a bike again. I even took a used silver 1100 Yamaha out for a test ride. I still have an M class license. I even took a thousand bucks with me to give the guy as a deposit but while I was out taking if for a test drive I realized that it was too solitary of an activity and I would miss my wife too much because she doesn't like riding on the back of a motorcycle. I figured that every moment I was on the bike by myself was a moment that I would not be with her. That and the 10 grand it would have cost to buy the bike, insurance, helmets, chaps, jacket, boots, etc, etc. I finally decided on my way back to return the bike that it was too selfish for me to buy so I canned the idea as I drove into the driveway and told the guy sorry. When I had a bike years ago it was my primary transportation and I was a student and I was single when I bought it. You gotta start thinking like… .

Before Frank could finish Mark interrupted, "Frank, don't give me any lectures on family right now. I just don't fuckin' need it." Mark groped to change the topic. "I've got a raccoon living at my place. Damn thing keeps digging in my compost dragging sloppy stuff around making a mess. She's living in my lawnmower shed. That is enough family for me man. Damn thing. Scares the crap out of me at night every time I go in the backyard. She sits there in the dark where I can't see her. Then all of a sudden she moves, she hisses at me and dashes off because I get too close. Gets my heart jumping every time. Damn thing.

"All I want to know from you is if you happen to have a live coon trap I can borrow? None of this family marriage stuff. All I can think about is that I gotta get rid of the beggar but I don't want to kill her. If I don't get rid of her she'll have babies in the spring and then I'll have a family of trouble to get rid of. That's all I need is a bunch of black-eyed bandits raiding my compost pile and digging in my little garden.

"If you don't have a trap then I guess I'll have to drive out to my uncle's place and see if he still has one I can borrow. He trapped one once. He used sardines as bait and caught a cat. Cat looked like a raccoon in the dark so he left it in the trap all night and called Animal Control the next morning. It wasn't until they arrived that my uncle felt damn silly. Turned out it was the neighbor's cat. He never liked the damn thing. Even though it stayed away after that, he figured it was a waste of good sardines."

"Sorry bud but I don't have a live trap for you. My neighbor said he used to have a live raccoon trap but he threw it in the lake — raccoon was still in it. Poor beggar."

Mark didn't show any sympathy, "I gotta get rid of my raccoon. It's driving me crazy, damn thing. I think I'll trap it and take it over to Ingrid's place and chuck it in her pool or kill it and hang it on her Harley." Mark laughed out loud, "I'm just kidding. I wouldn't kill it. I figure everything deserves to live. I don't know how some people can be so cruel. I might just have to spend the coin and buy a trap but I can't afford one right now."

Chapter 10

Therapy Excerpt – Prepubescent Sexualization

Mark sat with some crumpled notes, smoothing them over his lap. "So, Doc, basically I did a bunch of google searches like you wanted me to. There is a ton of stuff on "prepubescent sexualization." It wasn't hard to find stuff to read but I don't know about this topic that you wanted me to think about. I already know where you are going with this but I did my google project anyway."

Mark continued to press the papers into his lap. After an awkward pause he said, " The first thing that I came across was about pre-teen beauty pageants. Man there are loads of pictures of little girls all dolled up looking like sexy twenty-year olds. I can't believe the parents of these poor pre-teens. Turning them into adults like that. All I could do was laugh at some of the makeup and costumes. These pre-teen beauty pageants, for skinny flat-chested young girls, are nothing but a joke. They all look like painted dolls with padded bras. After I stopped laughing I was revolted or disgusted to see innocence stripped from a pre-teen girl that won't have a chance to naturally develop into a woman."

Mark shuffled threw his flattened papers, "After I read a bunch of stuff about the pre-teen beauty pageants and how destructive some people think they are to society in general, let alone to girls individual, I stumbled on the rantings by a guy about Pre-Teen Sexualization. He wrote a long essay called 'Pre-Teen Sexualization in Contemporary Society.' It was kind of boring but he basically says that he is struck by the growing gulf between public disapproval and the commercial exploitation of sexy images of young girls. He says that we have popular culture's sexualization of children pushed by the high profile commercial sexualization of pre-teens, especially in the modeling and music industries. He showed a bunch of semi-erotic exploitations of young girls and their unnaturally advanced sexuality. He specifically mentioned the Spice Girls and the hip swaying, pelvic thrusting that they built into their singing act. I think that what he was saying is not that the music, costumes and dance routines are so wrong, though he laughingly says they are ridiculously awful but his objection is that society tolerates them being sold and specifically marketed to pre-teens and that parents should be shot for allowing it. He feels that it is absolutely inevitable that the pre-teen, prepubescent target audience will inevitably mimic the product if they are exposed to it."

Doctor Waleed sat in silence taking notes while Mark crumpled away at his stack of papers.

"Oh, here is an actual quote from that guy. He said that, 'personally I think that the music is bad, the dancing is sultry and sexualized but sadly society laps it up like kittens at a bowl of warm cream. Everyone knows that eventually if you feed nothing but warm cream to a cat, long enough, you will kill it.'"

Dr. Waleed waited for Mark to pause and then interjected. "I have to commend you on your google search project. Now we have to analyze what you read and see how it applies to you and your relationships in general and specifically in relation to the sexual relationship that you had with your daughter. There is so much more work that has to be done."

Mark sat fidgeting with his papers pressed to his lap. "It is weird, it is all just weird. I feel like I am being given a long rope to hang myself. Not just given the rope but told to slip the noose over my head and even toss it up over a branch of the hangin' tree. It's just weird. I know you are trying to make me think that I did the same thing or worse to my daughter."

Chapter 11

Bottle of Scotch Talking

It was the Independence Day long weekend at the cottage. The wives, girlfriends and kids were already down for the night. The men; Dan, Mark, Harrison, Bobby and Jimmy, sat around a bonfire mulling over the meaning of life. The bottle of Scotch made its way around the circle three or four times in ponderous silence when Jimmy abruptly broke the spell with slurred words.

"Fuck man, it's not like you can help what fucking family you are born into and how fucked up you are going to get or who is going to fuck with your brain while you are growing up. Did you know that good old fucking Uncle Wally tried fucking with me when I was just little. He tried to get me to give him a blow job when I was about ten or eleven. He was drunk and waggin' his dick in the bushes taking a piss behind the cottage at the edge of the farmer's field. He called me a sissy boy and one day I would have a man's dick like his. He wagged it at me with a grin and said I should give it a suck."

Everyone just sat there in stupefied silence. Harrison finally broke the silence. "Is that just the whisky talking man. What are you doing making up stories like that after all these years."

Jimmy pulled the bottle to his lips and took another swig. "Yah it's the whisky talkin' but it is all true. I just stood there stunned shivering because I just got out of the lake and I was looking for my towel on the clothesline. He stopped pissing and pointed his manhood at me and dared me to touch it and come into the garage with him. He taunted me and started to walk towards the garage waving to me to fallow. As soon as he moved away I grabbed my towel from the clothesline and I ran away. Later he grabbed me by the hair and told me that if I told anyone what he said that he would cut off my nuts and turn me into a girl. I never told no one until this moment. He's an old man now and I finally figured out I don't have to be scared of him no more."

Bobby leaned over Harrison for the bottle of Scotch and took a long swig. "Uncle Wally did the same thing to me one year at the cottage. Who knows maybe it was the same year or even the same weekend. He grabbed my dick a few times when we were swimming. He laughed and I laughed and he made it funny like it was a joke between friends and then later he cornered me in the garage like he did with you Jimmy. He pulled his wiener out and had me touch it to jerk him off." Bobby took another swig. "He said he wouldn't tell anyone and he would buy me something special and what did I want?" Bobby took another quick swig. "He grabbed my hand and stuck his dick into it. I jerked him a few times and then heard a noise outside so I ran away. I never told anyone either, till now. From then on I just steered clear of him. Aunt Theresa always said he was a pervert and told the girls to say away from him. She should have told the boys as well."

"He was a classic sexual predator. I was wise to him. He was always scoping out someone to feel up." Harrison said as he reached for the bottle, wiped the spout with his sleeve as he took a quick swig.

"What do you mean he was a sexual predator? I don't think that I even know what a sexual predator is?" Mark put air quotes around the words sexual predator. "Those are pretty loaded words." Mark pulled out his cell phone and started to google. "It says here that: A sexual predator is a person seen as obtaining or trying to obtain sexual contact with another person in a metaphorically 'predatory' or abusive manner. Analogous to how a predator hunts down its prey, so the sexual predator is thought to 'hunt' for his or her sex partners. It seems weird that someone would actually hunt down their prey."

"There is nothing weird about it." Harrison said waving the almost empty bottle at Mark. "He sussed both of you guys out over time and tried to gain your trust. He even used being half drunk and joking with you as part of his hunting strategy. He went from friendly jokes to trying to get you cornered in the garage. You just had no idea of how long he had been planning his attack. I wonder who he did get jerked off by. You can bet he didn't try it on with just you two. What a fucker."

Mark pipes up and reads more. The dim blue light of his phone glowed in his scowled face.

"Sexual offenders recruit children by establishing a trusting relationship, for example spending time with them and listening to them. They may treat the child as 'special'; giving them presents and compliments. Offenders also use gifts and trickery to manipulate and silence the child into keeping the sexual assault a secret. This treatment can isolate the child from siblings, friends or parents. The offender may also establish a trusting relationship with the family and friends of a child, in order to have access to the child alone. When they have obtained the truth of the child and family it makes it much easier for the offender to sexually abuse the child. It is also important to remember that the offender often grooms the family in similar ways by buying gifts or helping out around the house as a way to gain trust from the family.

"There is loads more if you want to look it up but I figure you are all too drunk to care at the moment."

Jim poured another two-finger shot into his glass, took a swig from the bottle and passed it to Mark. Mark sat in silence remembering just how much further Uncle Wally managed to go with him. He choked on his all too vivid memory, scotch dribbled down his chin as he pulled the bottle from his lips. He was trying to remember what the present was that Uncle Wally gave him for his silence.

"Mark, you must have had a fucked-up moment or two in your life. Didn't you tell me years ago that some sexy woman down the street, that you did gardening for, tried to fuck you or something? You used to call her your Mrs. Robinson. How many times did she actually get in your pants?" Mark shrank further into silence. The shame of his Uncle Wally experience swirled through his Scotch-filled mind.

Dan snatched the bottle from Mark and taunted him with a high-pitched childish voice. "Poor Marky got fucked by the lady down the street when he was just fourteen, poor little Marky. Nothing even half as good as that ever happened to me. I saw my big sister standing in her bra and panties one time when I was about fourteen. I hesitated just long enough at her bedroom door, just open a crack, to get a good look and I went into the bathroom and pulled my wire. That's as close as I ever got to pre-pubescent sex. I was stuck with my virginity until I was about nineteen.

Mark seized the silent moment to stand up. "I don't know about you guys but I'm going to bed." He dragged himself up by the trunk of the tree he was leaning on, turned toward the long grass and peed. Staggering in the cool sand, in silence, he waved good night.

Chapter 12

Coffee with Frank – "Spotlight"

Frank furrowed his brow, "Mark, what are you looking so depressed about? You haven't turned the page on your magazine for five minutes. It's like you are stoned or something. You haven't started smoking dope again have you?"

"No I'm not stoned you idiot." Mark put down his magazine. I'm just kind of bummed out by this movie review. Ralph and I went to see "Spotlight" last night and here it is in the magazine and it I can't get it out of my mind. I have to say it's a movie worth seeing but it really bummed me out. Every sector of society will be shocked and the pedophiles in the audience will be relieved."

Frank put down his coffee, "I have seen clips of the movie on TV but what do you mean the pedophiles will be relieved."

"They'll be relieved to know that they are statistically not so much of an abnormality as they felt they were. Their shame will not be diminished and they will not be absolved by anyone in the audience, in fact they shouldn't let anyone know of their crimes as they might be lynched before they reach the dark safety of the street for a fast getaway.

"It's a wild movie. Get this, it presents the notion that 50%

of all Roman Catholic priests are sexually active and have broken their vow of celibacy and chastity more than once. If breaking the vow of celibacy includes abstinence from masturbation, as I think it does, then I would say that the numbers are even higher than 50% and there are a lot more liars in the priesthood than anyone might admit.

"And listen to this, for me the important statistic is that the movie suggests 6% of priests have committed a sexual act with a minor and now the media is suggesting that maybe the percentage is closer to 10% or even higher."

Mark tossed the magazine to the table and paused. "Totally aside from statistical analyses and debating whether it is 6 or is it 10% it has to be recognized that there are a lot of pedophile priests out there. The Roman Catholic Church, I am sure, would like to add the idea of 'past tense' to the idea that there are pedophile priests."

Frank chimed in, "Whether or not it is past tense for the Roman Catholic Church or not the media is dragging up scandal after scandal about sexual abuse committed by hockey coaches, Boy Scout leaders, teachers and the list goes on and on. They are all being dragged into the limelight."

Frank leaned forward with intensity in his voice. "I can't help but wonder how many unreported sex acts with minors there are still out there. I am starting to think that there are far more than reported. What sort of normal is society looking at? I haven't see the movie but I was reading that because of the movie 'Spotlight' a ninety-two-year-old man has finally come to the media and reported that 80 years ago he was forced to commit fellatio on his parish priest and had never spoken of it. Amazing that he never told anyone, till this day."

Frank paused to absorb the immensity and significance of it

all. "How many times has a man tickled the fancy of a 12-year-old girl and gotten away with it, the girl to embarrassed to say anything to anyone and maybe all he did was rub her privates with his knee as they played horsy. How many times at the family picnic has Uncle Harry, 'on purpose by accident' brushed up against his teenage niece and copped a feel or made a comment about her growing womanhood."

Frank scoffs, "As I contemplate this I'm starting to feel like it is an absolute norm. Not condoned but absolutely normal. How many times has a fellow-being simply thought it but never committed the act. How many times has an 18-year-old boy living at home with his ten-year old or twelve-year old sister or even fifteen-year old and taken advantage of her naiveté and touched her in ways that society would not condone. I am thinking that the numbers might be shockingly high."

Mark leapt into Frank's contemplative pause. "After seeing 'Spotlight' my warning to all of society is that if this movie teaches you nothing else it should teach you to never, never, absolutely never, trust a man to be alone with an underage child."

For a sense of drama Mark waved his hands in front of himself. "Let me repeat, 'absolutely never.' Never trust the priest, the Boy Scout leader, the coach or the teacher. Never trust the adolescent boy to babysit your daughter or your son. Never trust the police officer, the doctor, the dentist behind closed doors with your underage child. If more than 50% of priests are breaking their holy vow of celibacy after years of training and commitment to God then what percentage of your sexually active males, of any age, would take advantage of the innocence of a little girl or boy if they had a chance? For God's sake don't give a prospective pedophile the chance to turn into an abuser."

Frank slumps back in his chair. "The article I read suggests that we are all sexual beings including the adolescent child, girl or boy, looking for a sexual thrill. If you allow a man to be behind closed doors with a child then you are part of the problem."

Mark piped in and professed, "I still contemplate the idea that every form of sex, even with a child, is actually a form of making love. Even after all of these years of therapy, after my internal debate and the sex that I had with my daughter, I still wonder if it was mutually desired and a shared act of love. This unresolved internal struggle may be the end of me. I will either finally come to a level of acceptance of my acts or I will finally put the muzzle in my mouth and pull the trigger, pulled by the finger of remorse."

Mark and Frank sat sipping their coffees and reading in silence for the longest time before they folded up their papers, turned out of the coffee shop and went their own directions for home. The din of traffic filled the wall of silence.

Chapter 13

Therapy Excerpt – A Good Girl She Was

"You want me to talk about Rachel again? I can if you like but I don't see the point. She was just a normal girl. There isn't much more to say. She did just ok in school but she was way brighter than she let on to anyone. She just plugged along and didn't do much that was remarkable or brilliant but she was a good girl and wouldn't give anyone any trouble about anything. If you told her to finish her dinner, she finished her dinner. If you told her to go to bed in ten minutes, she went to bed in nine. She didn't argue with anyone about anything unlike her little sister, Selene, used to. Oh man she was the scrapper in the family. She learned that trait from her grandmother.

"When all of this started Rachel was twelve. She was tall for a twelve-year-old, tallest in her class and just starting to get boobs if you know what I mean. The top of her head came to just under my chin. I remember because her face pressed up against my chest when she gave me a hug. She was taller than her mother even at twelve. She would almost coo like a dove when I hugged her. The one thing that she had going for her was that she was real pretty and she knew it. Her stupid mother gave her a girl's make-up kit with blush and eye stuff and a lip gloss for her birthday when she turned thirteen. Right after she unwrapped it she took it into the bathroom, locked the door and came out twenty minutes later looking like a twenty-five-year-old, painted hooker. She looked about ten years older and everyone at the party, stupid idiots, said how pretty she looked and how grown up she looked. Her grandma Dorie even showed her how to do up her eyes better so she didn't look so much like a slut. I hated that stuff on her face. As far as I was concerned she was way too young for makeup.

"She never did understand why I didn't like her to wear the makeup when we went to visit my mom and dad. I just knew that they would not approve, and I thought she just looked pretty without any gunk on her face. One time when she was about fourteen or maybe a bit older my dad saw her wearing lots of makeup and made some comment about her being gussied up and looking like a tramp. She never wore makeup to their house again.

"Yah my youngest daughter, Selene, was the smart one and didn't care too much for makeup. It's not that she was a gay or anything, it's just that maybe her sister wore enough makeup for the two of them.

"Boys? Rachel? Yah she always had lots of boys hangin' around her at school even when she was twelve. I always had to keep an eye on her when she had friends over after school. I didn't want any hanky-panky going on behind my back. I know what kids can get up to when you aren't lookin'. I didn't want my girls to end up pregnant like my ex-wife did before we got married. My first wife and I got married in a rush so the bun in the oven wouldn't show at the wedding."

With exasperation Dr. Waleed interrupted Mark, "Do you

realize what you said a moment ago? You didn't want any hanky-panky going on behind your back. You know what kids can get up to. I let you off the hook so many times with things that you say just so you can continue on with your explanations of one thing or another but I think this time I have to stop you and have you examine what you just said."

Mark sat in silence with his arms crossed on his chest.

"I can, to some degree, accept that you might not have known, or fully understood, that the interference with a child's sexual development, by an adult, is wrong. I accept that it might have been good parenting instincts for you to oversee your daughter's activities with boys but how could you be so blind as to not draw the comparison between protecting her from boys and the need to protect her from yourself. You had to have seen that sexual interference with a child's normal progress involves a power relationship in which the abuser, in this case 'you', spoiled your daughter's innocence."

Dr. Waleed paused for a moment to calm his voice of judgment. "Maybe you are getting hung up on the word innocence as not being a valued state of being. Maybe we should look at the word innocence in relation to purity or virtue or even spotlessness. For us to make progress you have to see that tampering with a person's purity is a malicious self-serving act. I am sorry to say that our time is up for this week but think about that idea that tampering with your daughter's purity was a malicious self-serving act. We will continue there next week."

Mark got up and left the office without saying a single word.

Chapter 14

It's All Just a Bunch of Psychobabble

The wall heater thunders to life. Hot air courses into the room. Morning light scissors in through closed drapes. A gray ceiling fan hangs motionless over Mark's bed collecting dust sending long shadows across the ceiling. Mark reluctantly creeps into consciousness.

Leaning forward over the bathroom sink Mark pushes his anemic face towards the steamed mirror and rubs his hands over his morning stubble. He pulls down on his cheeks looked past his tired complexion into bulging red eyes. He is oblivious to his hand-written note that is stuck to the mirror. "Think Positive. You Will Make It. It's Only a Matter of Persistence." The note is curled, faded, spotted; God only knows how long it has been ignored morning after morning.

In a low grumbling voice Mark pokes at his teeth and mumbles, "We're all afraid of something." Toweling steam from the mirror he stuck his tongue out as far as it would go, looked down to his tonsils and rubbed his neck. He squints his eyes and continues with his habitual morning ritual of talking to his reflection in the mirror. He says, with whining cynicism, "My shrink says I'm afraid of finding out that I am sometimes malicious and self-serving and that I am full of justifications and rationalizations. Man that is a mouthful. Supposedly I'm afraid of finding out just what's holding me back from making a real commitment to any woman. It might cause change and change can be painful he says. Fear of the unknown. Hell, it all sounds like psychobabble to me."

Mark rolled his eyes slapped his cheeks continued on with his one on one diatribe. "Mark Beetleman you are pluggin' along nickel by nickel, worrying about every penny, wondering what you did to deserve this so-called sorry life that you live." He rocks his shoulders back and forth and rubbed his face again. "I have three failed marriages under my belt; Mary, Rose and Ruth. My shrink says that I'm still clinging to my second ex-wife so much that I can't move more than two blocks away from her. Damn, I spent my last penny to buy Mary a lawnmower but then what did I bloody well do for fuck sakes? I also cut her grass. Why the hell I didn't just give it to her 17-year-old kid to push is beyond me?" Mark thumps the side of his head with the heel of his hand and rolled his eyes at the mirror.

With quick, agitated strokes, Mark slashes at his stubble with his new, sports car-sleek, red Schick razor, guaranteed-to-make-any-women-want-to-kiss-his-baby-smooth face. "My shrink says I was looking for – 'come back to me pity points'. More psychobabble if you ask me. Can't we just do something good without it having a hidden agenda? Next time I won't tell him if I do something kind and generous for my ex. I'll just tell him when I do something spiteful and mean. Next week I'll just make something up and see what he has to say about that. I'll tell him that I do good things for people because I am compensating for having had sex with my daughter. That'll make his wheels spin. He'll think I'm making progress and he will be delighted."

Mark rubs the mirror with his wet hand and steps back from the sink. Still only half-shaven he points at the mirror. "It's my job. That's what keeps me here, not my ex-wives and it sure as hell isn't Ingrid. She can go fuck herself. It's my job, nothin' but my job that keeps me here. That's why I stick around this place, not because I want to get back with my ex-wife. Besides, it wouldn't matter, she doesn't want me anyway. I can't see that changing, even if I wanted to, which I don't."

Mark leans forward with hands on the cold white porcelain and looks himself straight in the eye. "Which I don't!" He mumbled to himself, "I'll move back to my hometown when I'm good and ready and not a minute sooner and meanwhile I'm damn proud of my job." He shrinks back down to a normal posture and almost whines. "I finally climbed two rungs up the ladder but I still always feel like I've got one foot on the ground stuck in the mud. Why is the damn ladder so damn slippery?"

Leaning back from the mirror Mark points back at his reflection, "It's the system. That's what it is. You can't only have bosses; you have to have grunt workers at the bottom and lots of them and even plenty of them sitting on a shelf like cans of peas waiting to be used. I used to be one of those cans of peas when I worked in the warehouse. Heck I still am a grunt worker even if I do work in a cubicle at a computer now. I just got a raise and a bit of respect from my boss, but I'm still a ground level grunt worker wishing I could earn enough to buy a house instead of renting. What on earth am I doing wrong? All I want is a house, a garden, a car and a family to come home to after a long day of work. What I want is a wife. That's why Ingrid left me. Because I'm dirt poor. Why the fuck would she leave a gorgeous house with a pool to move into a dump like this. My daughters moved hundreds of miles just to get away from me. What the fuck did I do wrong with my life?"

Bringing the towel to his face he sniffs at it, wrinkles his nose, sniffs again and tosses it into a growing pile beside the door. Slashing at his face Mark finishes shaving, splashes "Old Spice" on his face and then into his arm pits and mumbles, "Before my brother found out about me and Rachel he wanted me to move back home. My brooottthhher wanted me to get half of the money out of my ex-wife's house. My brooottthhher wanted me to move to his little flea-bitten town, come over for dinner twice a week and live happily ever after. My brooottthhher wanted... what my brother wanted was for me to rent a truck and move. I can't afford to rent a damn truck, let alone start looking for a job in a totally different state. Besides that he won't even speak to me right now, so fuck that!" Mark reaches for the tossed towel and dries his face.

Mark slams down the handle on the toaster and resumes mumbling to himself as if Frank was standing beside him. "Afraid of success, my shrink said, or was that afraid of failure? I still don't understand the bloody difference. It's just more psychobabble to me. How about afraid of not paying my rent? I bounced my rent check last month because I was five bucks short. Now that's real – there's no psychobabble in bouncing a check.

"Holy crap, look at the time. I had better get in gear. Maybe if I stopped going to the damn shrink I could afford to rent a truck and move. Maybe after I get a raise." Mark jots down a note on a scrap envelope pulled from the recycle box and placed it on the table just before he slams the door behind him. 'Don't forget to take out Rose's garbage tonight.'

Chapter 15

Coffee with Frank – Celebrate the Beauty of the Naked Child

Mark and Frank sat for their weekly coffee at a new outdoor café. Main Street traffic was not too noisy on this Sunday morning. Frank impatiently tapped his coaster on the cool glass table while he waited for his decaf coffee and Danish. "Frank, from what you say, I guess you think, that I think, that it is not even possible to celebrate the beauty of the naked child form in our modern culture without there being some level of titillation of spoiled innocence and the objectification and sexualization of children."

Frank smirked at Mark. "You try so hard to sound smart Mark that you just end up sounding stupid. I think that I agree with what you think that I think about the titillation of spoiled innocence and the objectification of children but what a lot of mumbo jumbo man. Let's stop your linguistic dance and cut to the chase. Do you know the wonderful painting of two young girls standing naked in front of a glowing hearth? You know the painting that I mean. Is it by Paul Peel? Even if someone hasn't seen it in a gallery they must have seen it in a magazine or even an advertisement."

"Yah, I know the painting you are talking about. It isn't two little kids standing naked. One of them is sitting on the floor, but you only see them from the back you idiot. Yah I've seen pictures of it."

"It's a painting of two little kids but it's really a painting all about innocence. It is such a famous image that it is now part of our cultural iconography. I think the title is 'After the Bath'. It is a perfect example of what once was an image of innocence, goodness and virtue. My point is that an artist could not get away with painting that image these days. Back in the late 1890s there were a lot of paintings of naked children. They portrayed innocence in a way that you could not get away with today. Now-a-days you would be tossed in jail on childhood pornography charges. Basically we live in a really weird culture when it comes to matters of sex or nudity of any age. Nudity simply translates as sex these days. It didn't used to be that way."

Mark laughed at the idea of being tossed in jail for painting pictures of naked children. "Yah I know the painting you are talking about but when did society change? When did children become something different than expressions of innocence? From what I can gather from studying history, cherishing childhood is a pretty modern concept. Totally aside from sex and nudity, young people were expected to pull their own weight as soon as they were able to walk and carry and be of some help to the household."

Frank sipped his coffee and paused, "In the old days I don't think that kids were even an expression of innocence. They were loved like family members but they were simply future laborers for the family. Girls probably did the same work as their mothers from the moment they were able to walk, and the boys worked like their fathers the moment they could escape from the apron strings of the mother, out of range of that romantic hearth that Peel's naked girls stood in front of."

"I'm not a sociologist," said Frank, "but I bet men had sex with children at an early age back then. I'll bet it was just a normal stage of growing up. So basically what is now considered an egregious act by a pedophile, against a young girl was, back then, a normal journey into being a young mother.

"My Great Grandmother was pregnant when she was just 14. My grandmother said that no one even tried to hide the fact of who in the family the father was. She just had 'his' baby. Everyone knew who the father was but they just buried their heads in the sands of tolerance and didn't stop him from coming to the dining room table for family dinners. Rumor has it that even his wife knew that it was 'his' deed. That's just how it was back then. Stuff like that was simply tolerated."

Frank squirmed in his chair. "I am glad I didn't live back then if incest was just tolerated and swept under the carpet. Some might say that incest has been frowned on because of the most obvious consequences of inbreeding that generally leads to a decreased biological fitness of a population. At least that is what I was taught in high school about inbreeding. Even though that might be true, my feeling is that incest between father/daughter or brother/sister was outlawed not for biological stability but because of the social moral implications. The worries about the deleterious biological consequences of incest is, I suspect, the lesser problem compared to the degradation of society. I guess incest has been around for a long time and I am not sure it is going to disappear any time soon.

"For some reason I had almost this exact conversation with

my buddy John the other day. He was saying that history has some very famous examples of incestuous relationships. He was talking about Caligula in Rome, having sex with his sisters, being one of the most egregious. However, the Bible is full of brother/sister, father/daughter couplings. He was reminding me that even the story of Adam and Eve has an unspoken second generation coupling between siblings. After all who did Cain marry? Who did Abel bed? Who did Seth know?"

Frank laughed, "I don't think that any of this was ever talked about in my Sunday School class when I was growing up."

Frank laughed again and shrugged, "How did we get onto this topic anyway? It is your fault, you brought it up. Now you've got me spouting on a philosophical tirade. One can't look at incest or pedophilia without looking at the questions and implications of what is moral law and what are the consequences of breaking moral law? Which comes first, moral law or legal law? And then one has to look at natural law and what constitutes cultural law? It takes me back to my university days of arguing a point in class. How do all of these laws blend and overlap? It's almost too much to fathom."

Mark put down his bran muffin. "You are right. It is too much to fathom. What's the point of hashing it over and over? Every male basically thinks with his dick. Society would like to think that the male libido is held in check by cultural mores but it really isn't. Those cultural values are shattered by images on television, in popular music, in teeny bopper magazines, in ads all over the place so what is the point of even discussing it."

"Mark, don't try and get out of taking responsibility for thinking with your dick. Not all men are the same as you. All the women that you are with week after week qualifies you for being morally infantilized. You make it sound like you don't know the difference between cultural disapproval and cultural approval. You know you don't get my approval for your life style with adult women let alone what you did with your daughter and I doubt that most men, would approve."

Chapter 16

Coffee with Frank – What's this Business about the Burkinis?

"Where do all the frickin' flies come from?" Mark waved three flies from the rim of his coffee cup. "At least when the coffee is hot the damn things don't try drinking the hot coffee and drown themselves if they fall in. I think that the heat keeps them away but they still land on the rim of your cup. I can't stand it." Mark feigned a shudder and wiped the rim of his cup with the serviette and continues his complaint. "I wish they would bug off. I guess that is the price we pay for sitting at an outdoor patio." He placed a coaster over his cup and pushed it away.

"Have you seen the news lately about this 'Burkini' business?" Frank shooed a fly with the back of his hand and put air quotes around the word burkini. "It's crazy. Our society has gone nuts. They are trying to outlaw them in some parts of France. They are trying to ban women from wearing them on the beach. The issue is making its way all the way to the French Supreme Court. Bloody well had better get stopped there. No one should have the right to tell a woman that she has to go virtually naked in public if she doesn't want to. Dorothy and I were in Turkey last week and saw what looked like a Muslim family on the beach with us."

"What do you mean you were in Turkey last week? You say that pretty casually. When were you in Turkey for Pete's sake? How long were you there for? Didn't we have coffee last Saturday or was it the week before?"

Frank scowled. "It was almost three weeks ago that we had coffee at The Red Skipper. I had to go to the Istanbul head office to make a presentation about our new project so Dorothy came with me. We had a great four days. We were buzzed out on Turkish coffee by the time we got home. I didn't sleep the entire way home. Anyway we were on a beach one afternoon and saw this Muslim family and the wife had one of these new designer burkinis that we have been hearing about on the news. It was so foreign looking that it looked like something out of a science fiction movie. It was this gorgeous metallic aqua colour with white beaded work all over the front of the top. It had a hood that was pulled up over her hair. Every square inch of her was covered except for her hands, feet and face. I personally think that they look hideously uncomfortable but I can't believe that anyone would try to outlaw them. What's this world coming to? She was all covered up from head to toe but you should have seen him. He had a belly of ample girth that hung down over his skimpy bright red speedo bathing suit. From the front you could hardly see he had anything on. They had three kids that were all frolicking in the water, all with normal swim suits on. I wonder what age they will make the nine-year-old girl start wearing a burkini like her mom? Can you imagine all of a sudden having to wear a sweat suit with a hoodie when you go swimming?

Mark perked up and put down his coffee and slipped the

coaster back on the cup. In a bit of a raised voice he blurted, "You're a nutbar man. What people are outraged about isn't that the woman's body is all covered up. They are outraged that it represents a poisonous ideology of repression against women." Mark violently flailed at a fly. "Some people, and I'm one of them, think that women have the right to wear whatever they want on the beach and even go topless if they want and yah you are right, what about the little girl of that family? Do you think it is right that some man will one day force her to abandon her pretty bikini and abandon the bliss of the sun and waves on her skin? Do you think that it is right that she will have to give up that freedom? The brothers will be allowed to grow bellies and man-boobs and go virtually naked just like their dad but no, not the little girl."

Frank furrows his brow, "You can say what you want but at least until the Muslim society changes and gets to be more progressive the burkini is a good solution. At least they can go to the beach and swim. Can you imagine swimming in one of those full black body bag burkas." Frank laughed, "I think you would drown."

"Yah", Mark sputtered, "you nutbar that's the point. How would you like to be a woman and have to wear one of those garbs, a big black tent and have to totally cover yourself when in public. You might as well put a leash on her and control her every move."

Frank shuffles in his chair. "Don't call me a nutbar, you frickin' nutbar. There is a sign at the entrance to our park that says 'All dogs, large and small, must be kept on a leash.' The dog is a dog not a woman and no one wants to put a leash on a woman."

"They might as well be a dog. Roll over Rover and play dead and while you are at it wear this burka."

Frank stiffens up. "Let's not get too far off track here. We are talking about the right to wear a burkini on a public beach. We are not going to solve all Muslim women's rights in this one conversation."

"You are right," said Mark as he sat back in his chair and took a bite of his organic banana bread. "But let me say this one last thing. What appalls me is the way that Western women all around the world protested outside their French embassies waving signs confusing the issue. Any intelligent person knows that France's objection is not to the burkini, and its cousin the ugly burka body bag but the protest is a statement to the love of women, and is not a hatred of Muslims."

"Yah ok I got it," said Frank, "but it is absolutely offensive, now in the year 2016, when men with guns start policing what women should or shouldn't wear on a public beach. That should be the issue that we all rally against not that a woman is not showing enough skin. Whether or not a segment of the population belongs to a repressive, misogynistic culture which denies females power over their own bodies is a different battle."

Mark laughs, "Ok, one final final word and then we can talk about the weather if you like. You said we are living in 2016, but the issue is that the Islamists aren't actually living in the 21st century. Some would say that they have not even made it into the 20th century. The Victorian era was more progressive than the Muslim orthodoxy is today. Even in Victorian times girls were more than just breeding stock."

"So we survived a summer of drought. Thank God we ended the summer with a few days of rain. Even though it has been a hot dry summer the Farmer's Almanac says it is going to be a cold winter full of snow."

Mark sat back in his chair, "Last year we hardly had any snow."

Frank waved at a fly, "By the way did you ever borrow a trap and relocate your family of raccoons?" Frank took the coaster from under his cup and placed it on top.

Chapter 17

A Thread of Emails from Brother Harrison

Dear Mark, I still can't cope *with talking with you. It has only been a few weeks since I found out that you had been raping your daughter for some six years. As you know I am no saint but my head is still spinning, I send you these two emails so you know how messed up I am about what you did even though it has been years since you stopped. You should know that just about everyone in the family, including friends, know what you did. There is a varying range of reactions but the general consensus is that you should just stay away, maybe for a long time, maybe forever.*

I can't talk but I send my regards because I think of you often.
Harrison

Dear Michael

My head is spinning. I learned last week that my brother, Mark, had been raping his daughter, Rachel, for 6 years from when she was 12 all the way to 18. She is now 25. It has sent my head spinning in all directions. How is this possible that someone you loved and respected could be so depraved and you didn't have a clue what was going on? It is like finding a skeleton in your closet. Your Uncle Harry has been missing for twenty years, murdered by your aunt Mable whom you have loved dearly for years and had lunch with you every Sunday after church and she has been telling you that Uncle Harry doesn't come to lunch because he is just not feeling well and now you wonder really what happened to your missing pet Rover and start thinking that maybe Aunt Mable did him in after he scratched her nylons years ago. Everything starts to sound absurd. Maybe she eats live monkey brains and loves them with a bit of vinegar. I wish I could understand.

So how is that for a bombshell dropped on your day?

I hope to see you soon, I need to talk in person and see if I can make any sense of this.

All the best,
Harrison

Dear Harrison,

You are right, that is a bombshell. My God, what a shock but it is maybe better than finding Uncle Harry's skeleton in your freezer. First I thought that maybe you were pulling my leg. Thank you for sharing this with me, a sign of the trust and love between us. That is horrible, very sad that someone could do such a thing, break the bond of trust between father and daughter. There is this animal nature in us that if we are weak it gains power and overcomes us. I am afraid it is in every man. Most of us have demonistic thoughts in some way or another but we find ways to build fortifications to that beast. God helps in that, divine Love, we can't do it on our own. We have to turn to the divine somehow, even those who do not believe in a particular version of God. Maybe, one day, he will be forgiven for his actions, on this side or the other side of the grave. Aside from his dear beloved daughter, he must also be suffering for what he has done. Maybe he suffers in the name of redemption rather than suffers simply because of the fear of being tried in a court of law. When our wrongdoings hurt others, especially those we love, we are hurt, every one of us. He must have his share of suffering, for sure he must. Think of his suffering and forgive him dear friend, you do have that capacity.

Love, Michael

Chapter 18

Therapy Excerpt – Father was a bit of a Tough Cookie

"Hi Doc. I have been wondering when you might want me to talk about my father. You keep asking about my daughters and my ex-wives and even my mother but you never seemed to be interested to know about my father. He was a bit of a tough cookie sometimes. One time in my teens he punched me in the face because I was aggravating him about something. I can't even remember what it was but it was only teenage crap. He almost broke my nose. He turned and looked me right in the face with his fist raised, his eyeballs bulging red like the devil himself and said if I told mother he would punch me in the face twice next time. He would have done it too. I learned quick to keep my mouth shut. My older brother, Harrison and even my little brother Jimmy and I had all been molested by him and we all kept our mouths shut. Who knows what else he did and to who. I was too young to remember but Harrison said that our dad went to each of our beds and played with our penises a few times. Harrison said he just pretended that he was asleep and actually just laid there and enjoyed it. He said that he never told anyone until he told me a few years ago. Same with Jimmy. We never told anyone else as far as I can tell.

"Even though people thought that my dad was mostly a nice guy and a pillar in the church and a good salesman and a good manager all his life, he could turn on a dime. At the very least he could easily be argumentative and pugnacious. I could tell you so many stories about how grumpy my father was one day and then play with us the next but I don't know why you don't want me to talk about my father. He doesn't have anything to do with me and Rachel. My relationship with my father was totally different from my relationship with Rachel and Selene. My relationship with my daughters was near perfect but we talked a lot, laughed and when they were growing up we did just about everything together. We didn't have much money, but that's ok. No matter what money you have or don't have, you can't have everything you want and you sure as heck don't get what you deserve out of life, so sometimes you just gotta take what you think you deserve.

"Yah there were some good times. We used to go camping every summer for a couple of weeks. We never had a cottage but we had a trailer. On weekends we would go to my aunts' and uncles' cottages but for a longer holiday in the summer we went on road trips. My brothers and I were the ones who made the fire every day and went out looking for wood in the forest. That was the best part of the holiday. We would come back to the campsite with our arms loaded. Mom and dad didn't know that we would steal wood from other campsites where there was no car parked. It was a lot easier than dragging branches from the forest. I think that my dad must have known but he never let on."

Chapter 19

Therapy Excerpt – The Fly Sucked Dry by the Spider

"**Yah, of course I know what she was thinking.** I know exactly what she was thinking. We actually talked about it. You think that I don't know what is going on in my own daughter's mind? You think that I don't know what is good or bad for her? It is society that has fucked her up not me. She said that she enjoyed making love with me. She liked it. Is that so hard to believe that she liked it? In fact she even sought it out and even got jealous if I looked at another woman. If I had a girlfriend, I mostly had to keep the two of them apart. She always hated my girlfriends and tried to split us up.

"The true shame, of so called incest, is that society does not condone it and does not see the love and beauty of it in some cases. The true shame is that the child or even the adult child sometimes can't just move on to a new relationship when it is time. Like all relationships, they come to an end and sometimes it is painful. Like most people, I've had a few painful split-ups in my life but we eventually get over them. Some are more painful than others. The sad thing for the so-called abused person is moving on to another relationship, and that they always tell someone, and then like my daughter they are instantly caught in this disgusting web of shame that is inflicted on them that they can't get out of. The only way out for the child, even as a now adult, is to learn to hate the adult by calling it abuse. Instead they should just move on. But they can't because of the hideous web of hate that society has woven. They become the fly sucked dry by the spider. If they just kept it to themselves they could just move on to another relationship and not be fucked-up."

Mark sat in silence with his hands folded on his lap for a few minutes.

"Have you ever heard of Warren Farrell and what he said in his article in 1977 about the positive aspects of incest? Well basically, I can't remember exactly, but in an interview, he argued that incest could be a good thing for everyone involved. If I remember properly he said, that 'incest is like a magnifying glass and that in some circumstances it magnifies the beauty of the relationship, and in others it magnifies the trauma.' In an interview, he said, and I even remember it exactly '…but the inference is that all incest is abuse. And that's not true.' Between my daughter and me it was love and it magnified the beauty until society got involved and fucked it up and said it was wrong and dirty and called me a pedophile. I abhor that word. Pedophile. It implies such social disgust.

"'There is nothing good or bad, but thinking makes it so.' I can't remember who said that. Was it Shakespeare? Or I think it was Einstein? It doesn't matter because it is true. Incest is bad only because of what society says not because it truly is. My daughter, years after we moved on to other relationships and were fine with moving on and fine with our years of making love, and got along with each other just fine, eventually told her then boyfriend, and he flipped out. Because he was a trained psychotherapist, he convinced her that she was abused and fucked-up. I feel like I was thrown under the bus by my own daughter with her telling her boyfriend and by her believing what he had to say about our making love. He's one fucked-up individual. But I guess I can't blame him. He's just a product of society.

"I was reading stuff on the internet about incest like you wanted me to and there was this girl that said she was raped by her father for years and she was intrigued by being able to do adult things like having sex and knowing things that other kids didn't know. She said she loved being wanted and loved and she loved being the favorite of all her brothers and sisters. She learned at an early age that she had power in her sexuality, even at the age of eleven. She said that she learned to be sexy at an early age and it gained her attention, and attention gained her power. I figure that she must have been a smart girl.

"I'm not trying to say that what I did to my daughter was right or wrong but this girl kind of suggests that there is more than one way for a girl to react after sex with an adult. She even says that the true shame of being abused as a child is that if you don't feel about it the way you 'should' feel about it, people think you're fucked-up. She said that people want to pity you and when you don't give them anything to pity, they say you're as sick as your molester. It is all totally screwed up let me tell you. Nothing makes sense to me anymore."

Chapter 20

Therapy Excerpt – The Reluctant Pedophile

"The word, 'pedophile'," with a disgruntled frown Mark throws air quotes above his head , "is such a dirty word. I would hate anyone thinking that I am a pedophile. I even looked the word 'pedophile' up in Wikipedia. It said that a pedophile is a guy who has sex with a girl that is eleven or younger. Rachel was twelve and already growing from a girl into a woman. When we had sex the first time and the fact is we didn't have sex, we made love. Sex is somehow a different emotionally charged word than 'making love'. We made love like adults. It makes me sick to think that someone would fuck a little kid. They should be shot for fuck sakes and besides even if the label fit, it is not like I decided to become a pedophile and have sex with my daughter. It is not like it was a choice I made. It just happened naturally.

"I even abhor the idea of me being a pedophile. When I went to the Dominican Republic and saw an old white man walking downtown holding hands with a pretty, very young black girl, my skin crawled. It still crawls when I think about it. I wanted to go over to him and punch him in the face and spit on him. I want to take his Lolita and hug her and tell her that he doesn't really love her just because he buys things for her and feeds her well. It is the love that is missing from that equation.

And then I look back and wonder how I became this same person that society so despises. I look at the fact that I loved my daughter. If anyone wants to call me a pedophile then call me the reluctant pedophile. I don't know what made me this way. I even resisted at first. You could even call me the unwilling pedophile. I am just tired. I am tired of the whole thing."

Dr. Waleed sat in silence for the longest time while Mark composed himself, whipped tears from his ashen face and gathered his thoughts. "Mark, I know you are upset about the word pedophile and its implications. Let's switch gears for a moment and look at the implications of incest and how it is a different kettle of fish from pedophilia. I remember a couple of weeks ago you telling me about your conversation with your friend Frank and what he had to say about incest. I wrote some notes of what you said. Apparently Frank suggested that incest was outlawed because of the social moral implications rather than the harmful biological consequences to society. I want you to know that I agree with your friend that incest was outlawed for moral reasons not biological reasons. So one cannot look at both incest and pedophilia without looking at the issues of why we have moral laws and what are the consequences of breaking moral laws? We are just about out of time for today so over the next week I want you to give some thought to what are moral laws and how did they evolve. Look at the question of how are you different from monkeys that might have sex with their offspring or for that matter how has our society evolved even over the last fifty or one hundred year to the point that it is no longer appropriate for us to have sex with our progenies.

Chapter 21

Letters to Brother Mark

Letter 1

Dear Mark:
I have had a difficult past six months since learning of your moral infraction but I am sure it has been tenfold more difficult for you — at least I can only hope.

I have compassion and love for you, brother. While what you did was despicable, I am in the process of separating action from person and seeing your real true core as being a spiritual reflection of divine Love. You are a loving, caring individual. This has been difficult for me partly because of my own self-condemnation for things, thoughts, actions that I have committed in the past. You are a painful reminder of who I was, and who I could have been if I had taken another wrong turn and followed you down the same path. I condemn you because I condemn myself, brother. As you know, I was in therapy for a long time before and after my conviction of sexual exploitation and serving three weeks in jail. That therapy was of pivotal importance to my spiritual and emotional growth. I will push, no more, against your resistance that you need therapy. I hope you one day recognize the value of professional help for yourself even though you say you will never commit such an infraction ever again. I can understand your being so embarrassed that you would not even want to divulge your actions, even to a therapist stranger.

After I learned about your past sexual relationship with your daughter, I contacted a therapist and had two sessions to simply help me think through what it is you did and its impact on me, let alone the impact on our entire family let alone your daughters. He and I felt that these two sessions were all I needed. I have moved on without further assistance from him but my mind keeps flashing to years of you raping your daughter. I look forward to the day that I can look at you and not see a pedophile rapist.

You have probably received the package that I sent you with spiritual articles about 'the sexually abused and the sexual abuser'. I hope you will read them and find some spiritual growth through the contemplation of seeing beyond the abuser and the abused. Read them more than once, as I did. Write notes and study them as you apply the spiritual concepts to you and your daughter. I hope that we can, in the future, talk and grow back to something similar to what we had as brothers.

Part of my difficulty is looking past the lie that you presented to me for all of those years while you raped your daughter. I am angry that you lied to me, brother. I am angry that you could not come to me and confess when you had just the thought of rape and incest. I understand the difficulty of confessing rape to me, but I thought that we were close enough that you could have confessed the "thought of rape" to me. I am sorry if I failed you somehow in being so inaccessible that you felt you could not tell me anything; especially this.

I must go for now. If you want to reply to this letter that is fine. If not then I will wait for a time when you feel less threatened, less vulnerable, less bad about yourself. I tried to reach out to Rachel but she is pretty much staying away from the family and I don't think that she is interested in talking to anyone about the entire mess.

All the best
Bro

Richard M. Grove

Letter 2

Dear Mark:

Even though I have not heard from you it is still a difficult time for me to come to terms with who you are and what kind of relationship we can possibly ever have in the future. On a suppressed level, I simply find it neither all interesting nor remarkable but mind-boggling – and that is on the good days. On other days it is like a tragic news item that keeps flashing across the TV in my mind. You know how the news media likes to put almost irrelevant info into a news flash, like age and race? "A fifty-five-year-old white male of Gary, Indiana is convicted of 300 counts of raping his teenage daughter. This is a publicity stirring case," says the pretty young reporter standing in front of the camera with a big microphone pressed to her lips. "Some are calling for a death sentence, some call for castration; some call for both, but there is no one sitting on the fence of ambivalence." In the news flash in my mind I see you walking out of a huge courthouse down a long wide set of stairs in handcuffs with head bowed, led by police to a curbside paddy wagon. I can't seem to shake this imaginary newsreel that keeps flashing in front of me day and night.

Recently while trying to shake that image I was dragged into thinking of the World Trade Center towers crashing to the ground in New York City in 2001 and how many times it flashed in front of the entire world, in front of me, and how it is burned into my memory and then I remembered that you phoned me as the first tower was burning, before it collapsed. We were bonded, both gob smacked and speechless. We watched the smoke, the terror, with our phones pressed hot to our ears, stunned. And now as I sit here 99% recovered from that tragic event, I realize that you might have just pulled yourself off of your teenage daughter to watch that devastation; pulled your hard dick from her young petrified vagina, standing hard in front of the TV.

You might have just raped your daughter and had no idea the degree of devastation that you were in the midst of causing, or maybe you did know. For all I know, you might have thought that you were making love. You might have thought that it was wonderful and tender. I have no idea what you were thinking but you might have thought that you were having a gentle intimate relationship with your daughter but you were indeed actually the World Trade Center towers crashing to the ground; you just did not know it then. You did not know that your life, her life, my life, all of our dear family's lives, and more, were actually in slow motion free fall crashing to rubble, burning.

It has taken years for your crash to happen and the dust to settle, and now the cleanup is hopefully beginning. The Twin Towers took hours to crash and burn, for the dust to settle and for all of the victims to be counted, it took weeks, months and still its aftershock is rippling through fragile minds as PTSD – post-traumatic stress disorder. It took five years for the new building to be erected, finished in 2006 but still the ripples of PTSD are being felt. Sadly, so sadly, I am afraid that your crash and burn, for your raped daughter, for your un-raped daughter, for your other victims, including those who simply liked and loved you and trusted you, it will take much more time to heal for all concerned than simply removing tower rubble and building a new tower.

The imaginary newsreel still flashes in front of me, brother; the handcuffs digging into your wrists, your puffy red eyes staring at your feet. Tears of fear dripping to the cold concrete stairs, salt stains of regret – regret that you did what you did, raping your daughter for years, or is it regret that 'she threw me under the bus when she told her boyfriend'; a quote from you, brother. Which regret do you have in your heart, brother? Which are you most afraid of?

This is what I need to know from you, brother, before we can have any kind of relationship. Are you full of remorse for what you did, angry at yourself for fucking your daughter for six years or do you still feel like you have been thrown under the bus by your daughter because she divulged the horrific acts to her boyfriend? This is the hinge brother, the crux of your possible redemption. You have to figure out what it is you are sorry for. Phone me when you are ready to tell me.

Bro

Letter 3

Dear Mark:
The sky is gray today, the heavy under-belly of clouds hangs low like my gloomy dark mood. It is trying to rain. There is little to no wind to stir the branches that hang over our back deck. The bird feeder is busy with thrashing blue jays tossing seed to the ground as they greedily flail for the choice, black sunflower seeds with little regard for others. Everything else is tossed to the ground. A coo of mourning doves flutters casually to the ground pecking at the spilled seeds in the belly-high grass, undisturbed by the chaos of blue that rustles overhead, the recipients of their flailing. It is quite an interesting metaphor.

I was thinking that this would be a great photography day. Moody skies dragging through tree tops. For a moment I was wishing that you were here with me to go for a walk to the edge of the lake and shoot the lapping shores like we had done so many times in the past. Whenever I have a question about photography, I instinctively reach for the phone to ask you about aperture settings, f-stop, shutter speed, ISO. You are, in so many ways, the smart one of the two of us. You always have been, brother. You just seem to know stuff. I have always said that you are a smart guy. You are a smart guy about all kinds of stuff like computers and computer programs. It is way easier for me to phone you and get an answer than to look anything up and read and read and figure stuff out. I have always *wished I was as smart as you, bro. As you know I am dyslexic, reading has always been difficult and slow for me.*

I have often thought what personality trait I would trade with you to be a good, fast reader? Now that I know the truth about you and who you really are and what you are capable of, what you have done with your life, that it turns out that you were, are, a pedophile, a rapist how is it that I could possibly trade any part of who I am for a part of you. Which part of you might I end up with? I will simply be happy being who I am. There is no point in bargaining with the devil. He will always have something up his sleeve. What bargain did you make with the devil? What part of you did you swap for a sexual thrill?

Bro

Chapter 22

2 Emails to Michael from Harrison

Dear Michael:

My mind is not spinning with the idea that a person can be evil. We have all seen movies or even met the individual that we think is a psychopathic animal where they are all bad with not a glimmer of hope of redemption. What my mind spins with these days is the how? How does the light and the dark live in a person, in the same mind, contemporaneously? How is it that the light shines so brightly and then the Mr. Hyde erupts into the mythical scream in the night?

Harrison

Email 2 just moments later.

Dear Michael:
I sit here and contemplate what I have done wrong in my life? As perfect and as high and mighty as I might think I am, I look at the moral infractions I have committed and wonder how I might have climbed so high onto the stool of judgment. I shock myself sometimes at how imperfect I

was, I am, or maybe will always be, and now I wonder how can I judge so harshly my dear brother for whom my heart bleeds.

My earliest infraction against a moral code, at least the earliest that I can remember, was when I was only ten. I stole twenty-five cents from my mother's coin box that held the treasury of the small but precious organization for which she was president. The punishment for this crime is that I still remember, more than fifty years later. The punishment is knowing the anguish that dear mother went through; counting and recounting the fist-full of coins, wondering how she could have miscalculated the tally. With humiliation tucked in the dark recesses between self-incrimination and a sense of stupidity, she turned to father for his calculations and then was finally left to dig in the depths of her handbag for the precious twenty-five cents to make up for her accounting transgression. She prayed that her error would not be recalculated one day by some officious treasurer more skilled than her.

I know that this crime of stealing a single coin might seem insignificant to my greater crimes but one fact that I know is that it sent me on the slippery slope of thinking that I could not only get away with an immoral indiscretion but that I could be absolved of my guilt through time. What was my dear brother's first crime against morality that let him slip into the pit in which he now surely wallows?

There is an important axiom that one needs to keep in mind about the slippery slope. Once you are on the slope, it is infinitely more difficult to gain your footing and climb up than it is to slip further down. Proud, at the time, of my accomplishment as a burgeoning thief, it became easy to graduate to bigger booty and even transverse from one type of moral indiscretion to another.

All the best,
Harrison

Chapter 23

Therapy Excerpt – 800 Years of Temptation

Mark was, as usual, slumped in the doctor's green, wing-back chair. He was getting tired of hunting and searching for meaning in the past. He was tired of the pain of looking at the history of his life. Breaking a long silence, the therapist leaned forward and said with a whisper of annoyance, "I keep hearing justifications and rationalizations from you. I think that you could convince yourself of just about anything and then try to convince me."

"Do you know the story 'The Garden of Paradise' by Hans Christian Andersen? Even though it was written in 1838 for children it could have been written just for you. Basically it is a story about temptation, but more importantly that temptation is laced with rationalization. Just like in his case the rationalizations finally failed, as rationalizations always do. In the end you will kiss the tears of the fairy of paradise and then pay the long painful price. In this act of disobedience to a promise, breaking a moral code, you too will be condemned to 800 years of temptation repeating your failures, time and time and time again. Until after all of those wretched years you finally learn, inch by inch by inch, how to overcome temptation.

"You can read the beginning of the story yourself but basically the crux of it is that the prince is told by the fairy of paradise that she is going to lay down and sleep under the tree of the knowledge of good and evil and the prince is not to even approach her, and to never kiss her no matter the rationalization that comes to him. She told the prince that even if she calls for him, to never come, even to her side. Even if she beckons him to kiss her that he should never, no matter what, ever kiss her. The prince is warned that he will be filled with temptation to disobey but he was warned that if he does kiss her the garden of paradise will sink into the earth, and the prince will be lost. The prince shrugged and assured the fairy that he would resist all temptation.

"Well basically as the story moves on, the prince was weak and soon found himself rising on one elbow from his sleep just to peek over at the fairy. After all what harm could possibly come of just one peek at her from a distance? Soon he was peeking for the second, third and fourth time and then as he was sitting up and leaning on the tree the prince thought, 'What harm could possibly come from me sitting and watching her at least just to make sure that she is safe.' After a while of watching to make sure she was safe, he heard her calling 'Come, come to me I am in danger.' Little did he know it was just the wind whispering through the branches. He reminded himself that he should not approach her, but just to make sure that it was not her calling, he stood and rationalized that he should listen a bit closer just to make sure. One step closer, two, three just to hear and see that she was safe and then he found he was standing over her arguing with himself that he will not be tempted to kiss her. I have not broken my vow not to kiss her, he argued to himself, 'I am safe to stay and simply admire her beauty but I will not, I must not go any closer.' As he stood over her inching closer and closer, a tiny tear formed in the corner of the eye of the fairy. It glistened like a diamond. It was so beautiful, he thought that he would only get closer to take a look at it. 'I will only look,' thought the prince, but a pure sense of joy filled him. Temptation, and then resistance, and then finally again temptation flooded over him even as he bowed just to look. 'I will not kiss her,' he rationalized, 'but I will only kiss the tear.' As he pressed his lips to the side of her eye he lingered only on the tear for an eternity and then finally felt her sweet skin on his lips and finally, ever so gently kissed her. As he pulled away a clap of thunder, loud and terrible, resounded through the trembling air. All around him fell into ruin. The lovely fairy, the beautiful garden, sunk deeper and deeper. The prince saw it sinking down in the dark night till it shone only like a star in the distance beneath him. Then he felt a coldness, like death, creeping over him; his eyes closed, and he became afraid.

"When he recovered, a chilling rain was beating down on him, and a sharp wind blew across his face. 'Alas! What have I done?' he screamed to the sky. 'I've sinned like Adam, and the garden of paradise has sunken into the earth.' He stood up and found himself in the depths of despair realizing that he had succumbed to temptation, inch by inch, inch by inch, with his ill-fated rationalization. He was now condemned to 800 years of temptation repeating the test of resistance over and over again until he finally mastered to never give in to temptation even for an inch."

Mark didn't even allow for half a second pause after Dr. Waleed finished his monologue. "Ok, I got the picture, you don't like what you call my rationalizations but for effin' sake, I'm dying here. You think that I'm a perverted pedophile, my family thinks that I'm a perverted pedophile, and society thinks that I'm a perverted pedophile. I might as well slit my throat. I don't know what I am but I am not a perverted pedophile. Who and what am I if there is no one that understands who or what I am? Does that make frickin' sense? If everyone simply labels me as a perverted pedophile then does that make it so or is that too much of an existential comment for you to understand? You are the doctor not me. All I want is to be understood." Mark put his hands over his tear-streamed face and dragged his fingers back and forth through his hair. A few moments later he stood and walked out of the room without a word.

Chapter 24

Therapy Excerpt – Mother

"So Doc, today it's going to be about my mother is it? Last time it was all about my rationalizations and justifications" Mark was tired and easily irritated today. Under his breath he said, "Whatever you say. You da boss."

Mark sat up a bit, "I had an ok relationship with my mother. It wasn't great but she was an ok mother. What more would you like to know? Like I told you once, she used to hound me about my clothes being too gray and my skin was too pale and I should go outside to play in the sun with other kids but mostly she just left me to my own devices while she drank with her sister, my Aunt Mary. The two of them used to drink straight gin with ice because it looked like water so no one knew if they were drinking or what they were drinking. They both put on bright red lipstick and painted their nails bright red and polished off half a bottle in no time.

"One nice thing that I remember about my mom is that she used to read to me when I was little; my dad never did. All he ever read was the TV guide. My mom used to read mostly little kids books from when I was just a toddler and grew into reading more advanced books as I got older. The last book she ever read to me was 'The Prince and the Pauper'. She noticed that I was actually reading along and I was waiting for her to turn the page and she stopped and told me to finish the bloody book on my own and pushed it at me. I think that she was dyslexic and a slow reader and when she discovered that I could read faster than her, she was embarrassed and decided that I could read myself to sleep from then on.

"Before she stopped reading to me she used to read 'The House at Pooh Corner'. She read it to me over and over again. I often wondered if she liked the book better than I did. She used to call me her Christopher Robin and rub the top of my head but I didn't like that much because Christopher Robin, in the story, has to grow up and leave Pooh and Piglet and Eeyore and move away and go to school and never see them again. I made her read some chapters so many times that I had memorized the words and I would say them out loud while she was reading. I never let her read that last chapter a second time. It just made me sad."

Mark crossed his arms sat in silence for a moment. His eyes turned red as he started to tear up. He rubbed his nose as if he had a nervous itch and continued after he cleared his throat.

"I bought that same Christopher Robin book just a few years ago when I saw it in a used bookstore. I haven't read a single word of it; all I have ever done is look at the pictures. One day I am going to find my own 'Hundred Acre Wood', if you know what I mean. I am going to finally find my place, and where I belong." Mark rubbed his nose again.

"So basically I have that memory of my mom and then there is this other memory that keeps creeping in that I wish I could just forget. One time when my mom and dad were having a big blow out she took me to stay at a motel out of town for about two weeks. She was so determined not to get found by my dad that we didn't go to Aunt Mary's place like we sometime used to. I don't know why she left Harrison with my dad, maybe because Harrison was older but she took me and little Jimmy. She packed a bag for the two of us and told my brother that Dad would be home soon and stay there watching TV. The three of us got in the car and drove outa' town. I guess she had a boyfriend and that is why they were having a fight and she was running away because he used to come over to the motel late at night when they thought Jimmy and I were sleeping. They would turn the TV on kind of loud and go in the bathroom and have sex. I knew what they were doing. Sometimes they left the bathroom door open a crack by mistake thinking we were both asleep and I saw them naked and screwing, her bent over the bathroom sink and him pounding at her from behind. I guess the TV was supposed to drown out their moaning. They would have a shower together and be in there screwin' for an hour. Jimmy never saw anything, he was too little and was always asleep.

"In one way it kind of made me sick and angry that he was just fucking my mother and that is all he came for but I never said anything. I got turned on watching them fuck like animals even though I was just little. It turned me on that I was watching something they didn't know that I was watching. I remember thinking that he had a little dick compared to my dad."

Mark reached into his pocket for a handkerchief to wipe his brow. He cleared his throat and continued, "My mom and dad used to screw mostly on Saturday afternoons. I knew they were going to be doing it because they would tell us boys to turn off the TV in the middle of our program and we had to go outside and play. You could hear my dad talkin' dirty through the heat vents and the bed bangin' against the wall. They would go at it for only about ten minutes and then dad would come out all puffed up and smilin' with a clean shirt on and go to the bar for the rest of the afternoon. Aunt Mary would come over and they would get to doing their nails and sippin' gin.

"And that is about it about my mom. I've got other memories about my mom and the family, and shopping and stuff like that but those are the two memories about my mom that kind of sum up what I thought of her, she let men fuck her and she had a good heart and read me stories. She was kind and gentle and nice to me when I was little and she screwed around on my dad a few times but I figured that he deserved what he got for all the screwing around that he did. Mostly she was an ok mom.

"I am just happy that my mother never knew what kind of a person I really was. Apparently no one ever told mother and apparently Rachel told everyone not to tell her Grandma about what had happened. I am not sure why. I think that it is because Rachel loved me and didn't want to hurt me by telling her grandma.

"Yah I guess my mother loved me the way I was or rather the way that I let her think that I was. I guess that is what mothers do. They are blind to the truth sometimes."

Chapter 25

Coffee with Frank – Leonard Cohen and Donald Trump in the Same Sentence?

Mark and Frank sit in their favorite café for their weekly Saturday ritual coffee. Frank flails his newspaper in the air in front of him as he complains about the high price of gas. "For Pete's sake I paid $2.26 a gallon yesterday and the price at the pumps is up almost twenty cents over night. Why do we have to pay more for our gas than the rest of the country? The paper says our USA national average is $2.10 a gallon. It's just not fair. The price for everything is going up every time you turn around and they blame it all on the price of transportation. High gas prices means more expensive everything."

As Mark goes to sit down he grabs at Frank's paper that is still swirling in the air. "I just placed an order for our coffees. Sarah will bring them over when they're ready. Frank, you think that the price of gas is high now you should wait until Trump is sworn in and starts messing with the economy, then you will see high gas prices. I was reading a blog this morning that was comparing Trump with Hitler and that fuel prices skyrocketed when Hitler took power and then the German economy tanked. Oh man, don't get me started." Mark was already well into a diatribe that he wanted to avoid.

Mark grabs at Frank's newspaper again and misses. "Frank, I'm not sure I am going to survive this current news cycle. It seems to me it's so full of shit. Trump the devil incarnate elected president of the free world, versus the old man iconic of the music world, Cohen, the saint of Pop and Rock dies at 82. They are battling it out for attention in the media. I am already tired of hearing 'So Long Marianne' and I am sure tired of hearing what a misogynistic prick Trump is. Cohen was just as much of a womanizer as Trump but you don't hear the media harping on that. You wouldn't want to tarnish Saint Cohen's reputation now that he is dead. I bet the sales of Cohen's newest album 'You Wanted it Darker' are going through the roof. Why is it that everyone wants a piece of a dead guy? In Canada they worship him as a cultural icon even though they know in his early days he was as much of a womanizer as Trump."

Frank swished his paper at Mark and says, "It sounds like you have quite a big bee in your bonnet, which side of the bed did you wake up on?"

Mark interrupted Frank with a quick reply. "Let me tell you what side of the bed I woke up on. I woke up on, the give Trump a chance, side of the bed. I know that Trump is probably a total misogynistic, redneck, s.o.b. the way the media paints him but surely he isn't all bad. Don't get me wrong, I didn't vote for him but I also didn't vote for Hilary Clinton either. The entire country acts as if there are only two viable candidates running for president. I voted Libertarian again. Not because I thought that there was a chance in hell that Gary Johnson would be president but because we need an alternate voice shouting from the damn rafters to make sure the government doesn't run rough-shod over the people. Fabulous, thank God our coffees are coming."

Mark pushed their things out of the way for the server and slapped his paper on the table and raised his voice, "The media is crazy. Do they really think they're going to hang Bill Cosby, Harvey Weinstein, Roman Polanski and Donald Trump with the same rope. The media is crazy. It is like they are on a witch hunt. Next thing you know they are going to hang Lassie for sniffin's some bitch's ass end."

Frank shakes his newspaper at Mark, "Oh man, Mark, you don't have a bee in your bonnet you have a bee up your butt. You are starting to sound like Trump spouting half-truths that don't make any sense. First of all I don't know Cohen's sexual proclivities or his past and neither do you but even if he was a womanizer it doesn't mean that he was a misogynistic blow hard like Trump. You can tell that Trump is a woman hater just by how he talks about women in public. Cohen's poems and songs were not at all about disrespect of women. You are just trying to paint them both with the same broad brush you have painted yourself with."

Frank slowly leans forward. In a low harsh voice he reminds Mark about his not so distant past and his non-existent relationship with his oldest daughter, Rachel. "I hate to bring it up again Mark but you can't compare Cohen's womanizing past with Trump without looking in the mirror first." Frank leans even closer to Mark. In an almost whispers he says, "You can't do what you have done in your life and not have been, and I think you still are, a misogynistic prick. No doubt you have some good qualities and that is why I still hang around with you. believe it or not I think you are redeemable. You are a good person in many ways but you still objectify women and you still haven't publicly apologized for your past deeds. Until you do you should keep your Trump and Cohen judgments to yourself.

"Every time you talk about Trump and Cohen and call them 'Misogynistic' I can't help but think about you bragging to me about you fucking this one or that one in your van and how many different sets of footprints you have on your van ceiling. At least Cohen went into a monastery and became a monk for years. I bet he became a better person. You can bet there was a lot of reformation going on in those years." Frank laughed out loud, "Maybe you should follow his example. Maybe you and Trump should join a monastery together you silly dweeb.

Chapter 26

Therapy Excerpt – Thanksgiving

Mark sat week after week in the infamous green, wingback chair; comfortable but not so comfortable that one would be inclined to be totally relaxed. Dr. Waleed sat in an identical chair facing almost directly across from Mark. "I have told you about my mother and father, about Frank, my brothers, my wives but you have never asked about my old girlfriend Jan." Mark rubbed the arms of the chair back and forth before he continued.

"Jan was just about the only gal that I was interested in for more than just sex. I had a strange conversation with her before we drifted apart. I don't know if she was fishin' for an 'I Love You' or what, but she looked me square in the eye and said, 'Mark, have you actually ever really been in love before?' I was a bit taken aback because we had never talked about love before and I am not sure that I wanted to. What is the point of talking about love? You are or you aren't I figure but at any rate she pushed me for an answer." Mark paused for a moment to let Dr. Waleed finish writing a note.

"Do you want to hear about this? I told her that my first wife, Rose, and I loved each other but we never actually said those three words. It started out as a bit of a game. Kind of like who's going to hang up first when you're dating and swooning over spending every minute with the person. She didn't want to say it until I said it and I didn't want to say it until she said it first because I knew she was playing this silent game of who speaks of love first. I think that I loved her. I wrote: I L O V E   Y O U ! ! one letter per square on the toilet paper one time and rolled it back onto the roll just to see if what her reaction would be. She never said anything. To this day I don't know if she just wiped her beav with it and didn't notice or what. How could she not notice bright red letters, big letters, one on each square? I wasn't going to ask if she saw the letters or not so to this day I've got no idea. Maybe all she saw was E YOU.

"Even on our wedding night all I could say was 'love yah' and all she said was 'right back at yah.' It's kind of like how I was raised. I don't ever remember my mom or my dad saying 'I love you,' or even 'love yah' for that matter. They never said it to me or my brothers for that matter. I can hear my mom saying – 'You don't need to say such things with words. I say "I love you" every time I wash your underwear and cook your dinner. You think I do that because I hate you? Don't be a bonehead.' I can remember her waving her spoon at me. 'You don't need smooshy words, you need actions.'

"I know I loved Ruthie, my third wife. She was a nice girl in a lot of ways even if she turned into a nagging bitch but I never told her either. That might be part of why she fucked all those guys behind my back, just to hear someone say, 'I love you'.

"I was at my girlfriend, Jan's parent's place for a Thanksgiving dinner about a year ago. I never smelled anything like it before. The aroma of roast turkey, mashed potatoes and yams greeted Jan and me as we walked into the warm house. Like I've told you, Thanksgiving has never been my favorite time of the year but this was kind of special. Holidays in general have always been filled with some level of consternation almost all of my life except for when I was little and didn't pay much attention to the fighting. I just can't fathom the mythical harmony that apparently revolved around some dining room tables and post-dinner antics. Telling stories, laughing over spilled milk, playing charades until you had a side-splitting stitch was not part of my family experience. At the very most, my family would watch a football or hockey game with a case of beer, or three. The men would get drunk and argue until they fell asleep. The women would take one car and drive us kids home. The men would show up in the middle of the night, chauffeured by the least drunk of them all.

"Even though I was not all that eager to go, Jan, wanted me to finally meet the rest of her family. Jan and I had been seeing each other steady for five, almost six months and I had managed to avoid spending what she would call, family time, with her parents, brother and sister. We arrived early and no one else had shown up yet. Jan is so nice. She put her arm around me and gently dragged me into the kitchen to meet her mom. After an awkwardly stiff hug, a short but polite exchange, it was suggested that I hang out in the family room for a while. 'I'm going to be with mom, helping in the kitchen.'

"Well that's about the end of the story really. I mulled around the posh but friendly family room. I sat and bounced up and down testing out a large cushioned armchair. I had never sat in such a nice chair before. The house was pretty nice. I just kind of perused all of the original paintings. Some of them were pretty nice. It wasn't till I was looking at all of the books that filled an expansive built-in wall cabinet that surrounded a large bay window that I knew Jan and I were not going to be together very much longer. She came from highbrow stock and I came from common people. It's like she grew up drinking champagne and I grew up drinking cheap beer or wine out of a box.

"I stopped and studied the photographs that paraded the fireplace mantel. It was crazy, I was flooded with memories, though very different from the history beaming from the smiling faces that stared back at me through the silver and black lacquered frames. I realized right then that I had no pictures of my daughters even taped to my fridge. Smiling faces of my estranged daughters only make me depressed. The few family pictures that my family might have are concealed deep in dusty disorder at the bottom of a cupboard somewhere in my aunt's, not so family, family room."

Mark sat quiet for a moment and then repeated his words. "…not so family, family room." Silence. "It is kind of strange to have a family room that is not all that friendly. I never really thought of it before but my family memories were more aptly linked to unscrewing the top from the third bottle of cheap wine, glugged by my father into mother's chipped, coffee-stained mug. I started to think that maybe Jan and I wouldn't even last another date. Unlike her group-hug-holiday-snapshots, memories in front of a glistening bronze turkey poised for carving, mine were of my father passing me a smoldering joint and telling me to take it into the other room to mommy."

Mark contemplated his past for a moment, "My Thanksgiving memories were not of family bliss, jokes told around the dining room table, 'pass the gravy' and 'more pumpkin pie anyone?' My Thanksgiving memories were of shattered plates slipped from trembling, inebriated fingers, stacks of unwashed dishes and squabbles over who was going out for fish and chips and another box of wine from Joe's wine shop beside the tattoo parlor. My memories were not framed in silver, tastefully placed on a mahogany mantel. Mine were framed in shame, guilt and fear, tucked away in the dark recesses of avoidance, glazed in anger.

"It's strange Dr. Waleed but the longer I stayed at Jan's parents' place the weirder I felt. I pondered the photos, one after another and picked one up to bring it closer. By then I was just sad. It was of a kindly, wrinkled old lady, smiling through the dappled shadows of a white sunhat. She had gentle wide eyes, an arm full of tulips pressed to her chest. For me it was unfathomable that this was a real person and not an image clipped from a magazine.

"Just as I was looking at this nice photograph, Jan walked in the room and said, 'That's my Nanna. She's the one that died about 10 weeks ago. I am sad that you didn't get to meet her. She was such a darling. I miss her so much. I used to stay overnight at her house when I was a little girl.' Jan took the photograph from me, smiled and placed it back precisely where it had come from.

"It made me sad to think that I had no photographs of the only grandmother that I knew. There may be some in a family photo album somewhere. I have no memories of what she looks like. I called my grandmother, 'G'. G for grandma. She was kind but distant. She was firm, rather than friendly. She was my only grandmother."

Mark stopped for a moment, shuffled in his chair as if uncomfortable, "I got ticked off at Jan when she offered me a glass of wine. I said, 'Why would you offer me a glass of wine when you know that I don't drink anymore?', even though it wasn't totally true but she didn't know that I was still sneaking a drink time and again? And then she offered me a soda and for me to go in the kitchen with her if I wanted to peel potatoes or I could just turn on the TV and see if there was a game on. She reminded me that her dad would not get home from golf with Denis and Deb for an hour. I guess I was just feeling weird or something because I made some comment about me watching a stupid game and I didn't play golf or something stupid like that.

"I just reached for the remote control, grabbed a cushion and stretched out on the long sofa bewildered by the mysteries of family bliss. I laid there for a while without the TV on wondering how different my life would have been if I had grown up in such a family with a sofa, uncluttered, untattered and the peace of mind to relax uninterrupted. What would my life be like if I was the one coming home from golf with a dad who cared? What would my life be like if I was the one to have a smiling, doting grandmother and a mother cooking a turkey?

Mark's mind wondered into oblivion for a moment, "I stayed there alone thinking. I knew that in the long run, one can only blame your past so much for the pain of the present. I guess I was not willing to look at the past, the present or the future with Jan. I kind of screwed up and let her go."

Chapter 27

Therapy Excerpt – Peanut Butter and Banana Sandwich

Mark replied to Dr. Waleed's welcoming question of, "How are you?" "I'm good, I had an ok week I guess. I got to see Frank a couple of times for a coffee but other than that nothing earth-shaking happened. Just the same old same old. I got a letter from my cousin Bobby that kind of fucked with my head for a day or two. I saved reading it for a couple of days until this past weekend. I was kind of afraid of what it might say, so I put it off. I took it with me for a walk when I went down along the Gary boardwalk. You probably know it, west along the lake towards Chicago. I like to get away from the smell of Gary industry sometimes so I head down there when the wind is blowing east."

Mark was unusually chatty and in a pleasant mood this week. "Everyone seems to smile with the bounce of joy in their steps when they are down there. It was a beautiful sunny day on Saturday so I packed a sandwich and drink and went for a walk. There were tons of people meandering with their kids, and boats in the distance listed only slightly in the gentle offshore breeze. It was kind of fun watching the greedy gulls bolt down french-fries tossed by laughing kids."

Dr. Waleed was starting to get impatient with the chit chat. "So what about the letter you took with you?"

"Yah I'm getting to that. I picked a bench that faced the sun, facing the lake. It was so cool sitting down there looking past the boardwalk to the soft-sand beach eating my peanut butter and banana sandwich." Mark laughed, "Yah I like peanut butter and banana sandwiches, I like the bread toasted and it's gotta be white."

An involuntarily smile twitched across Dr. Waleed's face as he thought about Mark's favorite food. He jotted peanut butter and banana sandwiches into his notes.

Mark saw him jot on his notepad and laughed again. "Sometimes mashed potatoes with lots of butter are my favorite, but they had to be smooth with plenty of milk like Billie's mother used to make – and they have to be hot.

"Well anyway, I swept the last crumbs to the pigeons cooing at my feet and read the letter. You want me to read you the letter? I got it right here." Mark pulled the letter from his shirt pocket and started to read.

Dear Cuz:

I decided to write a letter and lick a stamp because you have not returned any of my emails, maybe for as long as a year or more.

I was going to use the word 'slighted', slighted that you have ignored me but somehow that word has a bit too heavy of a connotation. I like the precision of language but am not sure that one single word will substitute.

My computer thesaurus gave me; ignored, neglected, snubbed, disregarded, omitted, spurned – nope – none of them will do on their own because none of them have the concept of caring built into them. Along with feeling slighted, I have a fear of intruding in your life if you truly don't want to talk to me, though I feel disregarded the way one disregards a telemarketer. Most of what I am feeling has to do with my caring for you as a cousin and hoping, trusting that you are well. We have not had an in depth conversation about life and happiness for a long, long time. We used to sit for hours and talk. I miss that, but now I am hearing some nasty rumors floating around the family about you and need to clear them up.

I missed you at the family reunion again this year, though some were glad that you had the good sense to stay away. It was held at Uncle Len's condo, so some of us went swimming. It has been about four years that you haven't come. Some in the family are actually feeling slighted by your absence, but they might not know about the rumor about you and Rachel. For me it's about missing you and hanging out with you like we used to. I miss riding my bike over to your place and then heading to the pond to catch frogs. I miss those days man. Being cousins is more than just sharing a last name, it's not even about blood and being family. It's about trust and being able to talk about anything even if you did something bad.

I guess you probably know that our cousin Drake passed on last year. I miss him loads; our cousin Nancy the year before that, both from cancer. My sadness goes deeper than just missing a person. It might sound like a cliché but it's not about the bond of DNA. I don't mean this letter to be melodramatic, but I feel like I am losing another cousin. We all have people slip through our lives like Jello off a hot tray. Zip, they are gone, and most often it doesn't matter, but the bond of the ones you love is important no matter what they have done.

Another Thanksgiving dinner has been had without you and another Christmas is around the corner. I hope we can get to see each other again before then, before Easter, before next summer, before one of us joins Drake and Nancy. I know we are older now and not about to go frog hunting, but we could get together and just hang out and talk.

I trust you are well. I hope you are happy. I hope to see you again soon despite anything that you might have done.

I hate to think that I have to come and hunt you down, Cuz. Write me or email me soon.

I love you, Bob.

Mark gently, almost in slow motion, folded the letter, slipped it back into the envelope and sat silently with his hands on his lap. Mark felt like the silence in the room was going to choke him.

"So what am I supposed to do now? Write him back, or just ignore him? Bobby is a great guy and all, but we've grown apart since our frog-hunting days. It isn't just him that I've grown apart from. I don't see or talk to anyone since they shunned me after they heard about what I did with my daughter. Even before that I started to stay away. I was so tired of everyone thinking of me as the poor orphan boy that lost his parents. 'Poor Mark, lost one parent to drink and the other to a stroke.' I've heard them talking behind my back like I was different after my parents died.

"The fact is that when my parents were still alive I liked family gatherings, but that was before they all found out about me and my daughter. I used to like family parties. I even liked helping my mom in the kitchen making pumpkin pies for Thanksgiving feasts but I guess that only happened once or twice. I like to pretend that it happened all the time.

"I liked visiting Gram's house with twenty-five or thirty people all showing up with fresh buns and butter, squash, yams, cakes and pies. I liked squeezing in beside cousins, aunts and uncles, plates on our laps, bumping elbows but I guess in reality it only happened once or twice. I kinda liked the fact that the women would be in the kitchen doing women stuff. I liked the tradition of the men hooting and hollering, gathered around the TV watching the Orange Bowl even if they were half cut and I liked rabble-rousing with my cousins in the basement. I liked everything, even if my dad drank too much and my uncles argued about hunting and gun control and too many trucks on the highway."

Mark leaned forward in his wing-back chair, "I remember one year we swiped the blankets from all of the beds to make forts between the tables and chairs in the basement. It was like an elaborate maze zigzagged through the entire big open room. One time we almost burned the place down with a candle one of the girls took into one of the blanket-slumped vaults. Oh man we were shocked back to reality when that happened. We got the fire out quick and we hid the burned sheet. It was like time stood still for those hours of fun and fantasy. It is funny that it only happened once or twice. I don't even think three times, but now all those times are gone.

"One year, when I was about ten, I was bouncing around the basement on a pogo-stick and banged my head on the low beam that ran down the middle of the room. They called me beam-brain for the rest of that holiday. Every time I walked into the room they would laugh at me and say, 'Duck Mark, duck.' I only half minded. Mostly I just kinda liked the attention, the belonging – but now all that is gone and it is all my own fault."

Mark scuffled his feet on the plush gray carpet in front of his chair. "What am I supposed to do?" Mark mumbled to himself rubbing his hands over his face. "How am I supposed to just pick up with Bobby as if it was yesterday? I'm happy just the way I am. I've got Frank and my job. I don't need anyone or anything else."

Chapter 28

Letter 4 from Brother Harrison

Dear Mark:

For years, you have been saying that you suffer from depression. I have empathized, sympathized and commiserated. I have felt badly for you and even worried about you committing suicide. I have phoned just to keep your mind occupied. I have sent txt messages with photos and emailed. I have prayed for you. I have offered some not so practical ideas of how you might overcome the effects of depression by sitting in the sun more, jogging more, taking up yoga or Tai Chi. I have suggested that you might change your diet, eat less carbs, eat less meat, eat less sugar, less salt, more sleep, all to no avail.

I have suggested to different people that they call you just to make sure you are alright and are not about to jump in front of a train, and now I wonder how much of your depression is simply symptomatic of being a pedophile for years. When did you start being depressed? I don't want to suggest that all depression is linked to being a pedophile or that everyone that suffers from depression will become or has been a pedophile. But man it must really fuck with your head, but maybe it doesn't affect you at all. Maybe you are just fine with being a pedophile and fucking your daughter for six years, but it sure is fucking with my head. It sure does cause me to be depressed. Numbers of how many times you raped your daughter over six years keep flashing in my mind. It truly is depressing, brother.

I put the Christmas lights up this week. I remember you helping me one year, both of us with frozen fingers because it was colder than usual that year. We always had fun doing stuff like that. It has been a while but after the lights were up, I guess it was a couple of years ago, you said something about being depressed and could not get in the spirit of Christmas. I just fluffed it off. I didn't want to hear anything about it. The lights were up, they were pretty, I was happy and I didn't want to know anything about your depression. For me there was nothing like Christmas lights to take away the blues, but it didn't seem to help you and now I am starting to figure out why. The wrongs that we do in our life are like a marble rattling around in a can. You just can't make it stop rattling no matter what you do. The wrongs that we do in our life just don't go away because we string pretty lights in front of the house.

Before I go I have to say one last thing about how smart you are but you sure are stupid. You use your smarts in all the wrong way. I looked up some stuff on the internet about what you did. The experts say that the reason pedophiles get away with their abuse for so long is that they choose their victims well. It's like you have a homing beacon that lights up when you find a girl that is lonely and neglected and desperate for love, and you found all of those things in your Rachel. You were able to seduce her because you gave her the very things she craved: attention, support, approval, respect and all the other things we associate with love. What I read also says that it works because sex is pleasurable and satisfying, even for a twelve-year-old little girl. It feels good from the inside out. It creeps most people out to think of a pre-pubescent child experiencing sexual pleasure, but they can and do all the time.

I gotta go. I probably said too much already. I hope you've read this over a couple of time and talked to a therapist about it – if you've finally gotten to the point where you're seeing one.

I hope we can talk soon.

Harrison

Chapter 29

Coffee with Frank – Tick Tick Tick

"**Oh man, Frank, I had a hard night last night.** I didn't get much sleep. I lay in bed trying to read. It's my habit to read myself to sleep almost every night. Well you know that, but last night there was a distant tick, tick, tick that distracted my concentration and I couldn't read and I couldn't even sleep. It just drove me crazy."

Frank perked up and looked over his paper at Mark, "Yah I know what you mean. It's like a dripping tap or the tap of a branch on a window on a windy night."

"Yah it's like that. I rustled loudly as I turned the pages of my book just to make some noise so I couldn't hear the tick tick even for a second and then I frumped my pillow and smoothed the sheets, all in an attempt to distract myself hoping it would go away. I was reading 'Lolita'."

"Lolita. You still reading that bloody book by Vladimir Nabokov? I thought that you finished it ages ago."

Mark patted the arm of the chair. "I just can't manage to finish it for some reason. I keep getting distracted by other stuff like last night I sat up and visually perused the room for the frickin' tick, tick, tick. I couldn't figure out where the bloody noise was coming from. I even talked to, Albert, my made-in-China, imitation English, white, green-eyed ceramic cat that was given to me when grandma 'G' passed on years ago, my only real friend by the way." Mark laughed. "Eventually I found the bloody ticking. It was this flippin' watch, my grandfather's watch that I wear every so often." He waved his wrist at Frank. "I slipped the flippin' thing into my top dresser drawer and returned to my book but by then I was too tired to read.

"By the way I don't want you to get the wrong idea about me reading 'Lolita'. It's not because it is particularly salacious or anything like that. In fact it's kind of slow and boring. I'm reading it because it was on the TIME magazine's list of the 100 best English-language novels and Ralph from work said it was a famous book from the mid-50s and it was a good read. Personally I have to tell you that I wish I had never started reading the damn thing but now that I have read so much of it I am determined to read all the way to the end.

"Even after I put the watch in the drawer I still couldn't read myself to sleep even though I was tired. I kept on thinking about Rachel and how she is still carrying the brunt of this sex stuff and I wished she was more like Lolita and just enjoyed it as part of her past and didn't get all fucked-up about it. If she is not careful she will carry it for the rest of her life.

"I was thinking about Lolita and she was just eleven when she was having sex with, Humbert Humbert. Humbert Humbert, what a weird name for a weird guy. He is the protagonist of the story, a thirty-eight year-old, literature professor and he liked young girls and he called them 'nymphets' all the way through the book.

"I don't think I am going to bother finishing it. I might

finish it just to see if Lolita is going to suffer like Rachel is suffering."

"What do you mean she is suffering?" Frank prodded.

Mark shrugged, "Well at least I figure she is suffering because she won't talk to me or even return my text messages. I was reading on line that a shrink was saying that Lolita will always question what love is and how to express it. Because Humbert was having sex with Lolita way younger than I was with Rachel, I figure that she could probably get over it a lot easier than Lolita or does it have to be like Lolita, that Rachel will be confused about sex and love and commitment for the rest of her life?"

"I hate to say it man but she'll probably have a hard time, even with therapy," Frank professed. "I hate to speculate about Rachel. I figure that she will make it just fine but it will take time. You gotta' give it time man. Everyone has to stop treating her like she is broken."

Chapter 30

Therapy Excerpt – The Top Drawer

"Hi Dr. Waleed. Yah. Everything's ok with me I guess. I'm not sleeping any better. One night when I couldn't get to sleep I put my watch in the top drawer of my dresser to shut it up and I got poking around looking for a packet of matches from the bar that a buddy and I went to a few weeks ago. As I was rummaging I wondered if everyone had a top dresser drawer of socks that was also a catch-all for the minutiae of life, you know what I mean, the bits and pieces that have nowhere else to go. Do you have a dresser drawer like that?"

Mark paused for about two seconds half expecting Dr. Waleed to answer even though it was a rhetorical question. "Does everyone have a three-year-old chestnut – dried and puckered; a few matchbox cars – scratched and worn from when they were five-years' old?" Mark smirked and said, "Some of my dinky toys have pink dots on the bottom and it reminded me of when I was little that all three of us boys would get cars for Christmas or birthday and my mother would put a pink fingernail polish dot on the bottom of mine and a red dot on the bottom of Jimmy's but Harrison, because he was older and didn't play with dinky toys much, his had no dots. This color code was to stop us from fighting over whose cars were who's. We never really learned how to share. Is that normal in a family that kids don't really know how to share?

"I was thinking about cleaning out that top drawer and then thought, not likely. Rearrange maybe but toss anything that is as important as a braided bracelet that Rachel gave me when she was just ten, or the handmade Father's Day card with a stick man picture of me standing between my two daughters.

"I figured it would be emotional suicide if I even looked too deep into the drawer let alone threw something out. Somehow even the dust and disorder were an important part of what I began to think of as a growing, ever-changing time-box; a walk down memory lane of better times.

"Well I mumbled and rummaging for a few minutes and finally pulled out a movie ticket stub from one of my last dates with Ruthie. I paused and remembered the gentle times I had with her holding hands in the dark of the flickering theater.

"What could I have done to make her love me more, to desire to keep our oath of 'til death do us part.' I just got angry and refused to lament so I jammed the ticket stub back in under the socks and closed the drawer. I figured no pain or pleasure is ever lost from one's top dresser drawer unless you let it escape, so I pushed it closed and didn't go into it, even for socks, for days.

"The desire to find that girl's phone number on the back of the matches just evaporated. I figured that I would rather sit at home with Ruthie rattling in my brain than feign interest in someone who was likely only going to be a one-night-stand. Sometimes it just has to be ok to take a painful walk down memory lane.

"Doc, I figured I must be getting old or something. That was the first time that I ever turned down the possibility of a one-night stand. I sat at home that evening and was starting to realize that there was just no relevance to my concept of time and history. It is all too painful. Time for me was like vegetable soup – all the little bits of my history were mixed up in the pot of pain, indistinguishably bubbling, gurgling away in a steaming cauldron of existentialism. For me it was hard to dip in and grab just one memory that I was happy to recount. I argued with Frank that there is no such thing as time if you don't have memories. It doesn't stand still, it doesn't zip by. It just doesn't exist. Well I know that my arguments didn't really stand up to scrutiny but I just did not know how to cope with the fact that I had no real fond memories of anything. A sliver of time, one slice at a time can evaporate into the hidden, repressed memories that are lost in the pot of soup we call memories.

"I just don't remember much from my past. I just kind of shut out time and history. Frank tells me all kinds of stories about his childhood, so I adopted them all. I tell colleagues at the office about the years of going to my family cottage on Lake Michigan – Frank's cottage, Frank's memories. He told me about his dad's bantam chickens in the shed behind his stucco house – Frank's dad's chickens, Frank's memories and I made them mine. His large sandbox, arguing with his brother over dinky toys – whose cars were whose – all his memories. I told them about finding a few of those dinky toys in my top drawer just the other day. He has told me so much about his great childhood that his stories started to become my bits of memories to cherish. Those slivers of memories actually became mine. I was having lunch with the guys from the office last week and they were telling each other stories about their childhood. One guy from Sri

Lanka telling us about his granny and her cooking and everyone eating together. Another guy talked about a pony he had and loved. I started to tell them about my years on the farm north of Chicago, along the lake and the big gray old barn we had there, but you and I know those were Frank's memories – not mine. I told them all about my marvelous childhood and the duck pond. The only time that I can actually remember events is when I find an object that triggers a memory. Do you have a top dresser drawer full of hidden memories?

"I couldn't think of anything fun or interesting to tell them about my life. It's full of fuck-ups. All I could remember were the years I lived in the basement apartment with my mom after my dad left us. I slept with my mom in the big bed except when she had a guy over and then I slept on the floor beside the fridge with my feet under the table so I wouldn't get stepped on. There was no room in the little bed that Harrison and Jimmy slept in. No light streamed into my life for most of those years. It's like one of those surreal scenes from a movie – my dad went out for cigarettes and never came back, but I sure didn't want to tell anyone at work that. I was getting ready to tell them about me, one of Frank's hitchhiking stories about crossing the country with a buddy and sleeping in a ditch, but it was time for us to get back to our desks. Like the fraud I am I skulked back to my desk and pretended I was happy pushing papers. Even though you are my shrink you don't even know the half of what I skulk about, and you never will. No matter how many therapy sessions we have."

Mark crossed his arms and slipped into silence for the last five minutes of the session.

Chapter 31

Email to Family from Harrison

December 27

Dear All:

It is 8 am, the morning after our family Christmas party. With blurry eyes, after a 5-hour drive home and a good night's sleep, I am compelled to start writing this post-Christmas letter and a pre-Happy New Year's greeting. I hope you like the attached pics.

We had so much fun playing the present game. Helen – you will be glad that I stole the book, "Edward Lear's Book of Nonsense" from you when it was my turn to steal a present. I will see who I can pawn it off on. Here are two highlights from the book.

> *There was a Young Lady whose eyes,*
> *Were unique as to color and size;*
> *When she opened them wide,*
> *People all turned aside,*
> *And started away in surprise.*

I will only inflict a second one on you.

There was an Old Man who supposed,
That the street door was partially closed;
But some very large rats,
Ate his coats and his hats,
While that futile old gentleman dozed.

I have to admit that I chuckled from cover to cover last night. I was too buzzed after the long drive home to go straight to sleep. If I am lucky I will find a twelve-year old with a bizarre sense of humor so I can re-gift it.

I wanted to say how great it was to see everyone yesterday, though obviously sad that some were missing.

Cindy, thank you for the meat balls that you containered especially for me to take home. I had some at the party and they were great as usual. Thanks. The best spice of all is your spice of generosity. Thanks for all of the presents that you added to the present game. It was lots of fun as usual.

As my family newsletter said, "It is great to be on the right side of the grass with you all." Nick and I sat together quite a bit at the family party. I learned the true meaning of that saying from him — thanks. Over the years he has always joyously said to me when I asked how he was doing, "I am on the right side of the grass and that's what counts." I am glad to share turkey with you all — thanks Betty for bringing the turkey, stuffing, etc.

Our dearest Selene, I am sorry you slipped into tears at the Christmas party thinking of your dad and how sad he is for missing family at this time of year for the first time. I tried to say in a only a few words to you; I am not at all sad that he is sad. That might sound unfeeling but this has to be part of his spiritual growth process, his penance, his reparation as it *were. Only in his aloneness will he suffer the consequences of his actions and this is a supremely good thing for his growth. I learned very late in life, I am still learning the axiom that there are consequences for all of our actions. Big and small actions have big and small consequences. Generosity of love was not his motive or his action. He must pay the price that others are and will pay, for his actions, for possibly a long time. Thank heavens we do not live in a society that believes in stoning. Family shunning is a small price to pay for his actions. Each of us are dealing with forgiveness, in our own way, at our own speed. Thank goodness divine Love still loves him. We will all arrive at the same place of forgiveness sooner or later, this life or next. Enough said.*

Jane, Rachel and Paul, we all missed you. We love you. It is only half of a party when not all of the family can be there. I hope you felt our hugs.

Aside from the food, the presents, the chatter, the clatter, the hugs, the highlight of the party, for me, was driving Little Lenny around in circles on his great-grandma's scooter. Can you still hear the squeals of joy reverberating in the foyer? I know some of you took pictures, can you send one to all of us? They have to go in the 'Happy-Spot Memory Folder' on each of our computers.

I am looking forward to a wonderful new year.
Happy New Year, everyone.
Harrison

Chapter 32

The Metamorphosis of Mark Beetleman

As Mark woke one morning from a troubled dream he swung his legs over the coffee table, stumbled past the kitchen and made his way to the bathroom. Holding the door jamb he groped his way to consciousness. Early morning glared in the speckled bathroom mirror blinding him to the bloodshot, talcum complexion that squinted back at him. Rubbing his neck he leaned forward straining to see his reflection. With trepidation he paused, wondering if he would see the metamorphosed exoskeleton of Gregor Samsa. As he slowly came into focus he was morbidly delighted to see his own gray, eye-sunken image staring back at him.

A full night on the sofa after reading Franz Kafka's 'Metamorphosis' is enough to give anyone a paralytic kink in the neck. He rolled his head from side to side. In his stumbling stupor he could hardly figure out what was dream and what was reality. He stopped for a moment and stared at the floor and scratched his head. Nothing was clear to him. What was a spillover from the terrifying book he still had rattling in his mind and what was the reality of his morose life. Elbows on knees he sat, painfully, slowly releasing, waiting, for the flow of relief.

Stepping out from his pajama bottoms he shuffled down the laundry-strewn, picture-less hall. Hands on both walls he fumbled his way to the bedroom. He flopped on his unmade bed. He covered his head with his stained, pillowcase-less pillow.

Within seconds Mark was stirring in fretful sleep again, staring down Kafka's giant beetle wondering if it would run from him or attack with its huge pincered claws. Standing on its hind legs, it stared eye to eye at Mark breathing the hot, rotting stench of hell in his face. Pincers rattled rhythmically, nervously twitching like a drunken butcher scything the air with a fist full of knives. Poised, motionless Mark stared deep into the creature's bloodless eyes, searching for his strength to stay calm. Cold sweat streamed from his terrified face; muscles ached with throbbing fear. He could see his own reflection in the shimmering shell of his nemesis. As it raised a silver claw slowly to his face he could see the cockroach had his same drawn and tired features, the same gray, sunken eyes. It stroked his face with cold steel, teary glass eyes. Unflinchingly, it pulled ever so carefully away. Crouched onto all six legs it scampered into the darkness and disappeared.

Mark jolted back to a fog-filled life, face buried in his sweat-drenched pillow. Sitting on the side of his bed the room spun out of control. Mark wiped the sweat from his brow. He stared at a new hole in his sock; the room still spinning. His untrimmed big toenail had scissored its way into open air. "I'm fuckin' pathetic," he said out loud to himself. "You aren't even motivated enough to cut your own damn toenails let alone get another job or even get rid of the damn raccoon in the backyard. Maybe your shrink isn't as stupid as you think. Stupid cockroach, you deserve every bit of crap that comes your way." Wiggling his toe he leaned over, yanked the sock off of his foot and apathetically tossed it across the room at an unruly pile of dirty laundry.

That was the last straw. In that instant Mark plummeted from depression into the dark depths of hopelessness. He was now more despondent than he thought possible. Three times divorced, stuck in a boring, unsatisfying job — and now a hole in his sock. Mark had slowly, one by one, let friends and social activities drain from his life. The only real friend he had left was Frank, but even Frank now had Dorothy.

In those early hours self-pity grew to be his only companion. It grew in Mark like black mold in a petri dish, smothering, eventually filling every crevice of his life. It felt to Mark like life was just not worth living. His discontent was more than the general malaise that had hovered in his life for years. It was now the constant unyielding consternation of self-deprecation. At this moment it seemed there was only one way out.

Mark reached for the revolver that he had set conspicuously on his night table some weeks ago. He jammed the cold muzzle into on his tongue. Pointing the barrel to the roof of his mouth he pulled gingerly on the trigger and stopped. The room spun. He toggled the hammer back and forth ever so gently. He wondered just how far he could pull the trigger before the gun would fire and it would all be over. He wondered if anyone would care. Mark gently released the trigger. The room spun out of control. With muzzle still in his mouth he wiped tears from his eyes and again pulled gently, just a little further this time and again gently released. Mark's eyes rolled to the back of his head. The room spun, he threw the fisted revolver across the room and fell heavy into his disheveled sheets.

Tossing, churning, sweat filled his red swollen face. Resigned to his task he groped his way to consciousness. He reached for a pen, pulled a note pad from a stack of papers and books strewn on his night table. He opened the note pad and waited for the right words.

Dear Mary: I have to take care of this one last thing before I leave. I have to apologize for being such a jerk. I have finally come to a painful realization of just how utterly selfish I am. When I was over at your place last week I took the last slice of the special raisin bread that you like so much. Even though I jokingly offered it around to others with my mock auction – "Going once, going twice, going... too late it's mine." I should not have taken the last piece. Even though I beat myself up over this I realized that I never apologized to you. I can't seem to help being a despicable cockroach. I tell myself over and over again that it does not have to be me, me, me – I am sorry. It seems that I will never learn – I will never learn. I am sorry. Mark Beetleman.

The room continued to spin violently. With precision Mark slowly tears the paper from the pad and with gentle care folds it into quarters. Pressing his hand across the final fold he stands the tented paper like a card on the night table where the gun once lay.

Shuffling to the corner of the room, Mark kicks a smashed lamp out of his way, picks up the flung revolver and sticks the cold steel muzzle back in his mouth. Penetrating the barrel with the tip of his tongue he is shocked by the acidic chemical residue. His pincer-like hands struggle to hold the slim metal revolver. Sucking air through the barrel the room spins, he slowly, ever so slowly, with deliberate hesitation pulls the trigger. This time all the way. The room stops spinning, he falls to his bed.

* * *

What day of the week is it? Is it a work day or weekend? Mark flicked on the small black and white TV that sat beside his bed hoping to catch the news and a clue. "Saturday. Thank God it's Saturday. What time is it?" Mark stretched for his flung watch that lay on the corner of his desk beside the broken lamp. With a long pause he frowned, grabbed the revolver and shoved it into the drawer of the night table.

"Great. Saturday and I still have time to meet Frank at Roasters Coffee Shop." Mark smacked his bare belly with both hands a few times enjoying the exhilarating smart. "Saturday. Frank. Pants. Pants, where are my pants? Living room." Dashing down the hall he popped into the bathroom, slapped cold water on his face, rubbed his wet hands back and forth through his hair and decided not to shave. "Ok. Shoes. Shoes. Where are my shoes? Hall, front door." Tucking in his wrinkled shirt he grabbed for his wallet and sprang out the door leaving it unlocked.

Huffing and wheezing Mark bounded into the almost full coffee shop and glanced around. "Frank, so glad you are still here. How are you doing? You been here long?" He dashed over and, uncharacteristically, gave Frank a quick squeeze; almost hug, on the shoulder. "Can I get you anything? It's my treat. I'll be right back. Hey, Sarah. How are you doing today? You look gorgeous, as usual. Have I ever told you that I love your auburn hair? Give me a Cappuccino today and one of those fruit and nut square thingies, oh and another one of whatever coffee Frank just finished."

"You sound like you are in a good mood today Mark. What's

up, win one of those lottery 'scratch and sniffs' that you are always desperately playing? I'll bring your Cappuccino and Frank's coffee over in a minute."

"You know why I am in such a good mood today? Well I won't make you guess. It's because I woke up just twenty minutes ago and found out I'm not a beetle and I'm just good old, fucked-up, Mark Beetleman."

Sarah smiled and smacked Mark on the shoulder. She pushed the plate towards him, "Here is your fruit and nut square. I always knew you weren't Ringo Starr or Harrison or even Lennon. Glad you finally figured it out." She turned and reached for another customer's coffee.

Mark whisked the plate from the counter and headed back to Frank. "Frank, have you ever woken up from a really realistic dream and found out you weren't dead?"

"What do you mean? I wake up not dead every morning and by the way what the hell was up with that phone conversation the other night? You really fucked with me you bonehead."

"Don't worry about that for now. I will explain later but you know what I mean. You have a totally realistic dream. You act out every part of it. Not a minute is missing in the dream and you actually shoot yourself. It is so real that you can even remember the smell and taste of things. Everything is in color and you wake up in a sweat and you think you're awake but you are actually still in the nightmare and you are dead. The room was spinning and spinning and you are just numb and you think that you are dead and then you slowly realize that you're actually alive and then you start to feel your head throbbing and you are almost glad you have a headache because it means that you are alive and then you slowly realize you are soaking wet with sweat and the room is still spinning and you have a really bad taste in your mouth and even that you are glad about because you are starting to realize that you are actually alive and everything is ok and you didn't actually kill yourself even though you are still fucked-up but still ok.

Frank puts down his New York Times and leans forward. "Mark, slow down, take a breath. You keep rambling on without taking a breath you're going to have a heart attack. No I've never had a dream like that. Sounds dreadful. That might explain why you look like you just fell out of the center of a tornado, but how come you are in such a good mood?"

"You know what kind of dream I mean? I've had smaller dreams like that all the time but less vivid, nothing like this one where even the room was spinning. I just woke up a half an hour ago from a dream just like that." Mark ran both hands over his head.

"Well that's just it, Frank. I'm alive and I'm not a cockroach. Yah I know I've been a cockroach in the past but have you ever read Franz Kafka's book "Metamorphosis"? I don't know what Freud would say about my dream but I've thought I was a cockroach all my life and sometimes I acted like one, but in the end I stared him down and he just skulked away. It was amazing. I dreamed the entire book last night and I turned into a cockroach just like Gregor Samsa and I woke up thinking that I was going to see me, me the cockroach, in the mirror but instead I saw me, my real self, still kinda fucked-up but just me."

From across the table Frank takes a joking swing at Mark, "And that's a good thing that you woke up as you?"

"Screw off" Mark said, "yah that's a good thing."

Mark sat back in his chair, "Chill out man, I'm just pulling your leg."

Mark tried to sit back and slow down, "I was never so glad

to be myself ever in my life. I can't believe it. I'm not a cockroach and I am glad to be me."

Sarah leaned over Mark's shoulder, "Here's your Cappuccino Mr. Lennon and here is your coffee Mr. Starr."

Mark reached up to take the Cappuccino from Sarah. "You're wonderful, lots of foam, just the way I like it, thanks. I should have a Cappuccino more often. Man, my shrink is going to flip out when I tell him about my dream."

Four scholarly analyses for book club analysis.

- A Journey into the Dark – *p. 137*
  by Brian T.W. Way

- From *Living in the Shadow* to *Some Sort of Normal* – *p. 141*
  by M.Sc. Miguel Ángel Olivé Iglesias

- ungeheures ungeziefer – *p. 146*
  by John B. Lee

- More To Think About – *p. 148*
  by John B. Lee

A Journey into the Dark

In Kafka's iconic short story, "The Metamorphosis" (referenced in *Some Sort of Normal,* Ch. 32 and elsewhere), Gregor Samsa awakes one morning to discover that, while his physical body has been transformed into a "gigantic insect", psychologically, he continues to exhibit emotional and intellectual capacities. In other words, he remains human. Even though he appears to be a bug, he remains human. He ruminates on his traumatic condition and reflects on the dreariness of his previous life as a travelling salesman and on the drabness of his room and the weather outside, and he feels hurt in being shunned by his family, yet he still feels "tenderness and love" and duty toward them. In the end, suicidally, he wills himself to death. Gregor's situation is pathetically echoed in the condition of Mark Beetleman, the protagonist of Richard M. Grove's *Some Sort of Normal*; as Gregor has been forced into his terminal carapace by his family's (and society's) parasitic greed, Mark Beetleman has arrived in his isolated (s)hell by enacting, and re-enacting, his own latent desires.

    Mark confesses to being an incestuous pedophile, of having had sex with his adolescent daughter repeatedly over a several-year-span; now that he has been exposed, in his own words, he is living a nightmare he can't shake. He is living that nightmare alone, except for conversations with his often-silent therapist Dr. Waleed; with an acerbic confidante named Frank; with his extremely narcissistic self; and with us, the reader. Mark finds himself cut-off from everyone about whom he really cares—his wife, his daughters, his brothers, his friends. His life has become a serial soirée of wives and lovers whose names he cannot recall.

Some Sort of Normal is Mark Beetleman's attempt to come to terms with his condition, with his feelings, with the meaning of what he has done and who he is. The novel is his soliloquy in search of identity, his "book of bosh", his "wheelbarrow full of horseshit" (Ch. 7).

Several canonical pieces of literature, from *Light in August* to *Death in Venice*, from *The Color Purple* to *Lolita*, from *God Help the Child* to *The End of Alice*, have broached the topic of incest and pedophilia and *Some Sort of Normal* joins that club, bluntly and ferociously. Grove's novel tackles this topic in its own unique way by abandoning linear narrative. Here chapter after chapter appear like random snapshots, pages of a disoriented, fragmented photograph album, all presented with a range of literary styles: traditional third- and first-person narrative, epistolary forms (letters and emails), diary and journal entries, and poetry—all effectively layered as a biographical palimpsest to capture Mark Beetleman's fractured life. In these, Mark revisits the actions and ideas that have led him to remorse, doubt and desolation, including an account of his ascent toward the original carnal act and his descent toward isolation and suicide after his behavior is exposed. In exploring such dark recesses of the human spectrum, *Some Sort of Normal* unfolds as a complex and fascinating fiction, a compelling read that sheds light into areas rare to the reader's eye.

Moral philosophers, from Socrates and Plato to Mill and Kant, have contextualized ethical principles—if one knows what is right, one will do what is good; Kant's categorical imperative affirms the existence of certain fixed moral laws and posits the rational idea that humans will shape their actions in alliance to those codes. But what if you know what is right and still do what is wrong? One begins to rationalize—what *is* right; what *is* wrong; according to whom? Mark grapples with the ethical issues inherent in his action as he sees them, and spins the wheel of blame from self, to daughter, to circumstance, to society, to differing historical norms, and even to the periodic vacillation of cultural morays. At times he seems honestly pleading his case; other times, he is the unreliable narrator caught in his own web of lies, maybe? He weaves in broken pieces a "beetle-man's" quixotic vision of the issues at hand.

At times, as reader, one is nearly seduced by his arguments, nearly buys into his salesman's lingo of prepubescent sexualization or adolescent desire, nearly forgives him his trespasses. Other times, not so much. By the final chapter, one thinks of Dickens as much as Kafka; like some kind of Scrooge discovering Christmas morning, Mark wakes from a hopeless and frightening dream and, in the end, forces himself into the realization that he is not a cockroach like Gregor Samsa. He simply chooses the froth of a Cappuccino over the acidic taste of the barrel of a gun. Now, for that choice to be credible, like those Dickensian heroes before him, he needs only to discover a benevolent heart.

The front cover of *Some Sort of Normal* shows a picnic table beneath the waters of a flood—whether the waters are rising or receding is unknown in much the same way, one supposes, as the state of "normal" is ultimately indeterminable. In

"The Garden of Paradise" by Hans Christian Andersen, a fairy tale referenced by the therapist Waleed (Ch. 23), a prince travels on a lengthy and dangerous quest to find eternal life in the original Garden of Eden. Once there, "on the very first evening" he succumbs to his human folly and weakness, relenting to his desire, kissing the princess and losing his salvation; Eden sinks into the earth forever beyond his grasp. Death then forces him from the spot "to wander about the world for a while" with the uncertain hope that he will find, far away in the future, a "happier life in the world beyond the stars". And so it is in the end for Mark Beetleman—like that picnic table in the flood, his is a flawed, imperfect life and 'some sort of normal' is the best he can have and, probably, the best he deserves. He is a bug after all, but he is human too.

Brian T. W. Way
Pedagogical scholar, writer, poet

From *Living in the Shadow* to *Some Sort of Normal*

Richard Marvin Grove takes us from his fictional memoir, *Living in the Shadow*, to his novel, *Some Sort of Normal*. Both books are poking a stick at the open wound of pedophilia that festers in just about every corner of our society. Both books by Grove are open to as many acts of judgment and interpretations as there are people out there lurking in the shadows.

My previous analyses on the main character, Mark Beatleman, from *Living in the Shadow*, made it clear that reading the book was hard, so very hard, because I have a thirteen-year-old daughter who is the light of my life. I had to detach myself, much against my will, from that fact, so I could read the book with a cool head and comment objectively, if possible, on its achievements as an excellent literary contribution.

In my previous review I do remember likening the brain to a box with electrical wires – an elementary but helpful comparison – wires crisscrossing in every direction (the synapses) and prone to maybe short circuiting at some unfortunate point in time and space due to a multiplicity of causes. Thus, in *Living in the Shadow* and in *Some Sort of Normal*, Beetleman´s acts might or might not be the result of his conscious and willing self, they might or might not be the outcome of a short-circuited brain. Is that Mark Beetleman´s case? We can only shoot in the dark with speculation – or perhaps shoot Mark Beetleman himself.

This new book by Grove, *Some Sort of Normal*, makes me feel as uneasy as his fictional memoir, Living in the Shadow. In being human, Beetleman has trespassed principles of decency. This is not normal in a moral society, but he jumps through verbal acrobatics to justify his acts of breaking the sacred realm: a father-child bond.

Psychological "deficiencies" may be the explanation yet never the justification to do evil, much less to try to validate such acts on a social level. Beetleman claimed it was an act of love in raping his daughter for years – my goodness! The fact is it was an act of manipulation, humiliation and depravation!

I found the opening chapter to be first-rate. The characters, compared to *Living in the Shadow*, are now more involved in dialogues, more in an exchange, helps me, the reader, flow along the confessions he is about to make. It sets the atmosphere of what is to come. More dialogue and added chapters are the variations from the original book, *Living in the Shadow*. *Some Sort of Normal* flows very well as a novel.

The way the main character, Mark Beetleman, presents arguments in his favor and blames everything, mainly society and the way he was raised, leads the reader, time and time again, to realize we are in the presence of a vicious mind filled with glitches. In the explanations to his dreams, he has done nothing but seek to hide behind a dirty, lame, self-excusing mask. However, it does not give him impunity at all to harm others, who are human and deserve dignity.

What remains to be seen is how deeply disturbed this man really is from a psychological standpoint. No one is above the holy laws – written or not – of ethics and affection and ironclad respect for one's children. Here the boundary is black and white, no shades of grey.

The image on the front cover is significant in many ways. It invites Freudian and non-Freudian followers into the enigma of why the table and its reflection. My first thought is to realize how isolated it is, how out of place in a peaceful and quiet setting. Its brown, mossy appearance underwater speaks to me of moral corruption. I can talk about the dirty boards, faded colours, and rusty bars, all of them images of dissolution and corruption. What did the author want to convey with such a family-picnic iconic image? What does the table stand for? Is it drowning or surfacing – or both, like the character's intermittent strife to survive beyond his acts and uncover some rationale, some defense to what he did?

Why the title "*Some Sort of Normal*"? Is it an invitation to peel layer after layer from Beetleman's warped mind to see if we can find an iota of "normal" in an abnormal man? Is it an invitation for the reader to look carefully at what is normal and just how normal are we all?

The final lines of the novel reveal Beetleman's effort to try to fit in and feel comfortable around people. "I was never so glad to be myself ever in my life. I can't believe it. I'm not a cockroach and I am glad to be me". Read between the lines, dear reader! The man is clearly stating how he feels! He is not an insect; he is a human – glad to be him! Once more, there is manipulation and a futile endeavor to be at peace with himself, and sell that notion to the reader.

Remember Grove's words at the beginning of the book: These are all "feeble justifications and rationalizations by the offender". Nothing more. Therefore, reader, parents, people of decorum and principles, beware!

Thank you Richard Grove. I welcome your new book on such a delicate topic. You laid it down in a new style, with a different voice that speaks to reach as many sensible and sensitive readers – minds and hearts – as possible. You have created a voice that skillfully states, reveals, prods, exposes and succeeds in warning and teaching in a skillfully balanced language for expert and layman, being in logical turns colloquial and technical according to the chapter and the contextual situation depicted by the author.

We can feel the painfully thorough research done by Grove for the book and his genuine urge and concern to reach people, to send a meaningful alert into the future.

I restate what I said in my comments on the original book: Richard, you have written a painfully dissecting, shocking story that needs – claims – to be told repeatedly, as frequently as these acts, sadly, repeat themselves; some made public, some struggling beneath the awful veil of silence and duress and impotence. This story stands as a red flag for parents, next of kin and our dear dear children. It will be difficult to forget this book. Ask the families and victims of such deviations.

M.Sc. Miguel Ángel Olivé Iglesias
Associate Professor, Holguín University, Cuba
Cuban President of the Canada Cuba Literary Alliance

ungeheures ungeziefer

Dear Mary: I have to take care of this one last thing before I leave. I have to apologize for being such a jerk. I have finally come to a painful realization of just how utterly selfish I am. When I was over at your place last week I took the last slice of the special raisin bread that you like so much. Even though I jokingly offered it around to others with my mock auction — "Going once, going twice, going... too late it's mine." I should not have taken the last piece. Even though I beat myself up over this I realized that I never apologized to you. I can't seem to help being a despicable cockroach. I tell myself over and over again that it does not have to be me, me, me — I am sorry. It seems that I will never learn — I will never learn. I am sorry. Mark Beetleman.

In the final chapter of Richard Grove's novel *Some Sort of Normal*, temporarily despondent, protagonist Mark Beetleman writes a confessional mea culpa expressing his regret for having been a selfish jerk in life. He'd awoken that morning from something of a grotesque nightmare torn from the pages of Franz Kafka's novella Metamorphosis. With a name like Beetleman, and with sins on his conscience that would make any of us feel akin to the cockroach of the mind, it is little wonder that Mark would wake in a cold sweat seeing his psyche as having something of an equivalence to that of a dung beetle. In that his letter to Mary, (more of a letter from himself to himself), contains the personal pronoun "I" eighteen times in a mere one-hundred and fifty four words, this reader humbly suggests that his effort to make amends is less a matter of redemption than it is a matter of suppuration of the sickness of the ego.

I'm reminded of Paul Bernardo's recent appeal for parole. According to the reports that I have read, this serial rapist, murderer spoke only mostly of himself and what he had learned. This is a sure and certain sign that he feels sorry for his fate rather than regret for his actions. What consumes the evildoer is self-pity, not self-awareness. And Mark's awakening involves the falling asleep of the insect within. What Beetleman sees in the mirror is the simulacrum of a human while shadow self, the daemon insectivore is the rationalizing of a mind erasing the past and putting the memory of his former self in a box he dare not open though it scratch the lid for want of freedom like a trapped beetle.

The cheery ending punning on 'Beatle' Ringo, 'Beatle' George, shares much with the foamy cappuccino of mental froth that masks the cup that shapes it. Richard Grove has written a complex and disturbing portrait of a man we suffer to know, a man who remains a stranger to himself. The eudemonia of well-being and self-realization will forever remain beyond his reach. In Beetleman's own words "I will never learn – I will never learn."

John B. Lee
Author of over 75 titles
Recipient of more than umpteen awards

More To Think About

http://www.parentingscience.com/sexualization-of-girls.html

http://manslife.com/8060/celebrity-child-molesters-pedophiles-jared-fogle/

Man's Life website
Many experts claim that child sex abuse **is cyclical**, and that up to 35% of abusers were once victims themselves. But at least some studies have shown that the cycle-of-abuse theory is **not sufficient explanation** for why people molest children. Recent research suggests that pedophilia might even be a **neurological condition** over which the afflicted have no control…

Either way, one thing is certainly true. The taboo nature of child sex abuse and pedophilia has resulted in a stigma that makes people very unwilling to confront its existence, and that is probably a bad thing. Indeed, there is a growing consensus in the scientific community that in order to stop child sex abuse, we need to **stop treating pedophiles like monsters**.

We know — this is a hard pill to swallow. Child abusers commit monstrous acts, but the frightening truth is that they are in many ways *just like the rest of us*. They are not creatures from another dimension. They are not demons. They are people. We can deny it all we want, but frankly, child sex abuse is a *human* problem. We need to start by acknowledging that fact.

http://www.nytimes.com/2014/10/06/opinion/pedophilia-a-disorder-not-a-crime.html?_r=1

CAMDEN, N.J. — THINK back to your first childhood crush. Maybe it was a classmate or a friend next door. Most likely, through school and into adulthood, your affections continued to focus on others in your approximate age group. But imagine if they did not.

By some estimates, 1 percent of the male population continues, long after puberty, to find themselves attracted to prepubescent children. These people are living with pedophilia, a sexual attraction to prepubescents that often constitutes a mental illness. Unfortunately, our laws are failing them and, consequently, ignoring opportunities to prevent child abuse.

The Diagnostic and Statistical Manual of Mental Disorders defines pedophilia as an intense and recurrent sexual interest in prepubescent children, and a disorder if it causes a person "marked distress or interpersonal difficulty" or if the person acts on his interests. Yet our laws ignore pedophilia until after the commission of a sexual offense, emphasizing punishment, not prevention.

Part of this failure stems from the misconception that pedophilia is the same as child molestation. One can live with pedophilia and not act on it. Sites like Virtuous Pedophiles provide support for pedophiles who do not molest children and believe that sex with children is wrong. It is not that these individuals are "inactive" or "nonpracticing" pedophiles, but rather that pedophilia is a status and not an act. In fact, research shows, about half of all child molesters are not sexually attracted to their victims.

A second misconception is that pedophilia is a choice. Recent research, while often limited to sex offenders — because of the stigma of pedophilia — suggests that the disorder may have neurological origins. Pedophilia could result from a failure in the brain to identify which environmental stimuli should provoke a sexual response. M.R.I.s of sex offenders with pedophilia show fewer of the neural pathways known as white matter in their brains. Men with pedophilia are three times more likely to be left-handed or ambidextrous, a finding that strongly suggests a neurological cause. Some findings also suggest that disturbances in neurodevelopment in utero or early childhood increase the risk of pedophilia. Studies have also shown that men with pedophilia have, on average, lower scores on tests of visual-spatial ability and verbal memory.

The Virtuous Pedophiles website is full of testimonials of people who vow never to touch a child and yet live in terror. They must hide their disorder from everyone they know — or risk losing educational and job opportunities, and face the prospect of harassment and even violence. Many feel isolated; some contemplate suicide. The psychologist Jesse Bering, author of "Perv: The Sexual Deviant in All of Us," writes that people with pedophilia "aren't living their lives in the closet; they're eternally hunkered down in a panic room."

While treatment cannot eliminate a pedophile's sexual interests, a combination of cognitive-behavioral therapy and medication can help him to manage urges and avoid committing crimes.

But the reason we don't know enough about effective treatment is because research has usually been limited to those who have committed crimes.

Our current law is inconsistent and irrational. For example, federal law and 20 states allow courts to issue a civil order committing a sex offender, particularly one with a diagnosis of pedophilia, to a mental health facility immediately after the completion of his sentence — under standards that are much more lax than for ordinary "civil commitment" for people with mental illness. And yet, when it comes to public policies that might help people with pedophilia to come forward and seek treatment before they offend, the law omits pedophilia from protection.

The Americans With Disabilities Act of 1990 and Section 504 of the Rehabilitation Act of 1973 prohibit discrimination against otherwise qualified individuals with mental disabilities, in areas such as employment, education and medical care. Congress, however, explicitly excluded pedophilia from protection under these two crucial laws.

It's time to revisit these categorical exclusions. Without legal protection, a pedophile cannot risk seeking treatment or disclosing his status to anyone for support. He could lose his job, and future job prospects, if he is seen at a group-therapy session, asks for a reasonable accommodation to take medication or see a psychiatrist, or requests a limit in his interaction with children. Isolating individuals from appropriate employment and treatment only increases their risk of committing a crime.

There's no question that the extension of civil rights protections to people with pedophilia must be weighed against the health and safety needs of others, especially kids. It stands to reason that a pedophile should not be hired as a grade-school teacher. But both the A.D.A. and the Rehabilitation Act contain exemptions for people who are "not otherwise qualified" for a job or who pose "a direct threat to the health and safety of others" that can't be eliminated by a reasonable accommodation. (This is why employers don't have to hire blind bus drivers or mentally unstable security guards.)

The direct-threat analysis rejects the idea that employers can rely on generalizations; they must assess the specific case and rely on evidence, not presuppositions. Those who worry that employers would be compelled to hire dangerous pedophiles should look to H.I.V. case law, where for years courts were highly conservative, erring on the side of finding a direct threat, even into the late 1990s, when medical authorities were in agreement that people with H.I.V. could work safely in, for example, food services.

Removing the pedophilia exclusion would not undermine criminal justice or its role in responding to child abuse. It would not make it easier, for example, for someone accused of child molestation to plead not guilty by reason of insanity.

The below text is an email from John B. Lee to the author Richard M. Grove in June 2016.

As I think of the notions of pederasty in contemporary culture, I am struck by the schism between public disapproval and commercial exploitation. On the one hand you have the high profile castigation of pederasty and on the other hand you have popular culture's sexualization of children, especially the music industry's Erotic exploitation of female sexuality.

Think here of Baby Spice (of the spice girls), Miley Sirus and Britney Spears, both of whom were child stars in Disney culture and both of whom parlayed prepubescent objectification of the underdeveloped female body, grinding it out in videos that were so explicit as to leave nothing to the imagination. Brook Shields broke down the taboo with the film Pretty Baby, and a young Jodie Foster in the film Taxi Driver made the sexuality of young females almost acceptable. Eye candy, Jail Bait, whatever you want. Calvin Kline underwear ads, heroin chic, and Lolitas and nymphets in visual arts.

Is it possible to celebrate the beauty of the human form in art without promoting spoiled innocence and objectification of and or sexualizing children. The statue of a young female naked in the harbour in Copenhaggen is either an example of the beauty of the female form or it is an example of the exploitation and promotion of the sexualizing of children.

This conversation is only possible among people of intelligence, mature and contemplative disposition, stable and healthy personal sexual development. We do not live in a vacuum. We live in a very weird culture when it comes to matters of human sexuality.

When I was in Ireland, we visited a museum of Celtic culture. In the time of the Celts, the life expectancy of a human female was somewhere in the mid to late 20's. Child bearing years for that matriarchy began with puberty meaning around 13 years of age. Of course, statistics are skewed by infant mortality and early childhood diseases that carried many people of in youth. Some Celts did live to a very ripe old age. That said, life was hard and notions of 'childhood' are cultural as much as they are a matter of chronology. Indeed, childhood is a very modern concept. Young people were expected to pull their own weight as soon as they were able to walk talk and carry. Girls did the same work as their mothers the moment they were able to walk, and boys laboured like their fathers the moment they could toddle out of the range of the fire without being eaten by wolves.

So, what is now "pederasty" was then puberty – sex – motherhood.

Incest is something entirely other. Incest has been frowned upon because of the most obvious consequences of inbreeding. Until recently first cousins often married, especially in nobility, but children born of brother sister couplings were so often genetic disasters as to make humans create laws (first moral, then governmental) against marrying your sister.

On the other hand, history has some very famous examples of incestuous relationships. Caligula in Rome being one of the most egregious. However, the Bible is full of brother sister father daughter couplings. Even the story of Adam and Eve has an unspoken second generation coupling between siblings. Who did Cain marry? Who did Abel bed? Who did Seth know?

What is moral law? What is legal? What is natural law? What is cultural? Romeo and Juliet were children by today's standards. Juliet was twelve or thirteen, in a time when nobility married off their daughters as soon as puberty struck, and sometimes before. Girls were marriageable as young as ten, though it was understood that the husband would refrain from visiting her bed before she had her first period. As soon as she menstruated, she was fair game.

We are animals, and if one observes the animal kingdom, at least in the domestic world, we separate dogs, cats, sheep, goats, cattle, horses, as soon as they begin to develop. And we introduce the stallion to the mare, the dog to the bitch, the tom to the feline, the billy to the nanny, the rooster to the hen, the cob to the pen, the bull to the cow, the boar to the sow, when the gilt, the heifer, the ewe, the jenny, are fully grown. Full sexual development and the capacity to conceive comes long before a person is fully grown.

The male libido is held in check by cultural barriers. Those cultural barriers are shattered by images on television, in popular music, in teeny bopper magazines, in ads at the mall.

So someone like your main character, who is somehow morally infantalized and lacks the imagination to understand that cultural encouragement is not the same as cultural approval.

It must be very strange for someone who thinks it is okay to have sex with a child to be told it is not when the images in popular culture encourage him to believe otherwise.

When one looks to the financial collapse in 2008 and one asks, "Why did no one go to jail?" The answer is quite simple (and incredibly complex at the same time). Because what was going on was not illegal, it was wrong, but not illegal.

When someone recently asked a particularly thoughtful person, "What is pornography?" That person replied, "I can't define it for you, but I can tell you this. Most people know what it is when they see it."

Some of us simply KNOW that the sexual interference with a child by an adult is wrong, indeed, it is evil (if you agree with me when I say that the definition of "evil" is this: evil is that which makes the worst from the best.) Sexual interference with a child involves a power relationship in which the abuser spoils innocence. To say that children are not sexual creatures is to deny an absolute biological certainty. To suggest for a moment that interfering with children because they are sexual creatures is okay is clearly wrong, it is an EVIL that has few equals.

Even a baby might play ice cream spoon under her diaper or a little boy might play wee wee with his pee pee. It does not translate that this is in any way an invitation to interfere with or violate the natural curiosity of little people.

I know you know all these things, and I know I know them, but we live in such a weird culture it sometimes helps to share our thoughts because otherwise we see the madness of popular culture and despair.

all good things,
your pal, John B.

A Quick Bio Note:

Richard M. Grove otherwise known to friends by his nickname, Tai, was born into an artist family in Hamilton, Ontario, Canada in 1953. He is now a Brighton artist, writer, photographer and publisher, father of two daughters, Rebecca and Sarah, grandfather to two grandsons, Lionel and Nico, married to writer/editor Kim. He is the Canadian President of the CCLA – Canada Cuba Literary Alliance – as well as the Founding President of the Brighton Arts Council.

He has had over 100 poems published in many different periodicals around the world as well as having been published in over 50 anthologies – the most recent Beyond the Seventh Morning and The Dream, The Glory and the Strife, featured

poems, prose and photographs. He is the artist and author of over 15 books including his most recent and infamous book Living in the Shadow.

He was an active member of the CPA – Canadian Poetry Association for almost ten years serving on the executive for seven years including five as President. Richard is also the founder of the Canadian Poet Registry, an archival information website that lists Canadian poets including biographical information, their book titles and awards. One can view this website at http://www.hiddenbrookpress.com/Registry.htm. Richard has given speeches, readings and workshops on poetry and publishing at literary festivals in Canada, Cuba, Germany and New Zealand.

Since graduating from Ontario College of Art, in 1984, Richard has exhibited in more than twenty, solo and group exhibitions in Hamilton, Toronto, Boston, Calgary and Grand Prairie. He has his paintings in over thirty corporate collections across Canada. Four of his most noteworthy photography books are: *Sky Over Presqu'ile, An Ode to Victoria Lake, North of Belleville* and *In This We Hear the Light.*

Photographs by brother Christopher

www.ingramcontent.com/pod-product-compliance
Lightning Source LLC
LaVergne TN
LVHW040059080526
838202LV00045B/3706